CONTEMPORARY AMERICAN FICTION

JESSICA FAYER

Award-winning poet, novelist, and short-story writer John L'Heureux taught high school for three years—in Fairfield, Connecticut, and in Boston, Massachusetts. Since then he has taught at Georgetown, Tufts, Harvard, and for the past eighteen years in the English department of Stanford University, where he is Lane Professor of Humanities. He has twice been awarded writing fellowships by the National Endowment for the Arts. Six of his other works of fiction —*Tight White Collar*, *Desires*, *The Clang Birds*, *Comedians*, *Family Affairs*, and his most recent, *The Shrine at Altamira*— are available in Penguin editions. He is married and lives in Palo Alto, California.

Jessica Fayer

JOHN L'HEUREUX

PENGUIN BOOKS

PENGUIN BOOKS
Published by the Penguin Group
Penguin Books USA Inc.,
375 Hudson Street, New York, New York 10014, U.S.A.
Penguin Books Ltd, 27 Wrights Lane, London W8 5TZ, England
Penguin Books Australia Ltd, Ringwood, Victoria, Australia
Penguin Books Canada Ltd, 10 Alcorn Avenue,
Toronto, Ontario, Canada M4V 3B2
Penguin Books (N.Z.) Ltd, 182–190 Wairau Road,
Auckland 10, New Zealand

Penguin Books Ltd, Registered Offices: Harmondsworth,
Middlesex, England

First published in the United States of America
by Macmillan Publishing Co., Inc., 1976
Published in Penguin Books 1993

1 3 5 7 9 10 8 6 4 2

PUBLISHER'S NOTE

This is a work of fiction. Names, characters, places, and
incidents either are the product of the author's imagination or
are used fictitiously, and any resemblance to actual persons,
living or dead, events, or locales is entirely coincidental.

THE LIBRARY OF CONGRESS HAS CATALOGUED THE HARDCOVER AS FOLLOWS:
L'Heureux, John.
Jessica Fayer.
I. Title.
PZ4.L685J4 [PS3562.H4]
813'.5'4 75-31970
ISBN 0-02-571650-6 (hc.)
ISBN 0 14 01.5224 5 (pbk.)

Printed in the United States of America

for my wife
Joan Polston L'Heureux

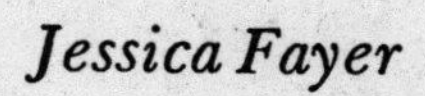

Jessica Fayer

1

Mrs. Fayer pauses at the corner of Charles Street, impatient for the light to turn. The two women she is following have crossed the street ahead of her and gone left and now she has lost them again.

She glances at the traffic light, which still does not turn green. She begins to panic. Perhaps the women . . . but then they reappear. They are looking at a display of old china in the antique shop just beyond the taxi stand.

She watches them, waiting.

Two young men are waiting, watching her.

They lounge against the bank, smoking cigarettes, watching the rich women pass by with their smell of expensive perfume and money. They watch Mrs. Fayer open her pocketbook and take out a lace handkerchief with which she pats her forehead and her upper lip. She has that rich look; she carries cash; they can tell. They watch her while she tucks the handkerchief carelessly back into the pocketbook and they notice that the clasp has failed to catch. She is a woman in a hurry, distracted. The best kind.

The light flashes green and one of the young men moves forward as if to follow her, but the other one touches his arm and gives a barely perceptible nod to the right. A security guard has come out of the bank to stand for a minute in the blinding sun. And so the two young men continue to slouch against the wall, waiting. They see a little girl point at the open pocketbook, and they see Mrs. Fayer snap it shut and test it. And then slowly, casually, they push away from the wall and amble down their side of the street. They look into all the store windows, they laugh and shove one another, but not for a minute do they lose sight of the woman. They are in no hurry. They are fifteen years old and have all the time in the world.

Mrs. Fayer is seventy-six years old and very nearly out of time.

She can see the women at the end of the block. She walks faster, but the pain beneath her ribs quickens, and she cannot catch her breath. She leans against the window of the drugstore to rest for a minute.

Across the street the two young men stand before the window of a hardware store, studying the reflection of the woman who has stopped for a rest.

It is an ordinary September afternoon in Boston and the heat rises like flame from the pavement. The windows without awnings are ablaze with light, but the drugstore window is shaded and Mrs. Fayer can feel the cool glass through the thin linen of her dress.

Mrs. Fayer is not certain who the two women are, but she thinks they are Mrs. Price and Lulu Mercer. She has seen them less than an hour ago having lunch at the Top of the Hub. Mrs. Price is carrying a parasol against the sun. Yes, they have to be Mrs. Price and Lulu Mercer. Nothing would make sense otherwise.

She moves away from the cool window and sets out again down Charles Street. She has lost the women for the moment, but her strength has come back with the little rest she has had, and she forgets her sudden rush of panic.

At the corner of Charles and Chestnut, she stops and looks up Beacon Hill. The women are old, they would avoid the hill. She crosses the street, walking rapidly now, only glancing in stores the women might have entered. She walks the length of the block and then another block.

She has lost them. She turns back. She will return to Chestnut and go up the hill.

Across the street the two young men pause at the window of a clock repair shop. They study the large display of antique clocks: there are sun dials and sand clocks and water clocks. And there are clocks with mechanisms exposed, hundreds of tiny wheels turning and turning against one another, interlocking, intermeshing for a moment, and then moving on in an eternal circle.

They light cigarettes and then, without looking either way, they step out into traffic. There is a squeal of brakes as a car lurches to a halt. "Goddamnit," the driver shouts, but he cannot be heard over the answering squeal of brakes from the car behind him. There is the crunch of metal as the second car plows into the first. The two young men do not bother to look. They stare straight ahead, knowing cars will stop for them.

But one car does not. A green Mercedes has come tearing down the hill and has turned onto Charles Street and now, as the driver sees the two young men step into the stream of traffic, he says, "Watch this," and presses harder on the accelerator. The heavy car bears down on the two young men. They are going to be hit. A woman on the sidewalk screams, her hand at her throat. And then, impossibly, the car has gone and the two young men, having jumped to safety, are shouting obscenities after it.

Mrs. Fayer hears the commotion but continues on. Charles Street is mad, hopeless; besides, she has a mission to complete.

"Mrs. Price," she says aloud.

"Lulu Mercer," she says.

At the corner she looks up Chestnut Street and then both ways on Charles. A policeman is standing outside the florist shop, and on an impulse she goes up to him.

"Two elderly women?" Mrs. Fayer asks him. "I wonder if you might have noticed them? One has lots of little curls across her forehead and the other one is, well, stout . . . with glasses. She was carrying a parasol. I thought, perhaps, they might have gone up Chestnut Street."

"Two elderly women." The policeman taps the palm of his hand with his nightstick and gazes over her head, thinking. After a while, he nods in agreement with himself. "Yeah, I think you'd be right trying Chestnut. Chestnut sounds about right to me."

"Thank you," she says, seeing he has no idea what she is talking about. And again she says, "Thank you."

"That would be your best bet," he says, pointing with his nightstick toward the top of the hill.

The green Mercedes squeals to a stop at the red light; the driver has seen the policeman pointing his stick.

"Mrs. F., you cute thing!" A beautiful black girl thrusts her head from the car window to shout at Mrs. Fayer. "How about a ride!"

The policeman looks at the girl and then at the woman and then back again at the girl. The girl is on drugs—anybody can tell that—but how in hell do you book her when Adam owns City Hall.

"I'm just walking, Martha," Mrs. Fayer says, "I'm out for a stroll." Her voice is formal and she turns rapidly away from the car. Adam, at the wheel of the Mercedes, honks his horn in greeting, but Mrs. Fayer does not acknowledge him.

As the policeman moves toward the car, Adam leans heavily on the horn and lets the car roll a few inches toward the crosswalk, straight at the two young men in the middle of the street. They stop, defiant, but then move on as they see the policeman switch his attention from the driver to themselves. The black girl shrieks with laughter. The policeman puts his nightstick through the open window and shakes it slowly at Adam. The girl stops laughing, but the policeman is not looking at her anyway. He levels the nightstick at Adam's chin and after a minute he says, "Baby, you just watch your fucking ass!"

"Yes, sir! Officer, sir!"

"Watch it, that's all."

"Sir!"

The policeman taps the green car with his stick and watches it pull slowly into traffic. A Mercedes SL sedan, he figures, must go for a good fifteen thousand. And he is right. Adam paid fifteen thousand for the Mercedes, paid in cash, the day after he cracked up his red Ferrari. The Mercedes, he has been told, is more sturdy. The policeman waits for the roar as the huge engine accelerates furiously and in a moment he hears it. He shakes his head. The kid is a born loser. He'll kill himself some day. Everybody knows Adam Brockway now that he has come into his money.

The policeman turns to look up Chestnut and sees the two young men across the street from Mrs. Fayer. Purse snatchers? She'd make a good target. You can tell she's got money by the way she walks. Tall and thin. Nothing flashy; the elegant kind. Could be fifty years old, could be a hundred. Beacon Hill money keeps you looking young. And those kids are trouble, no question. Should he follow them? Should he bother? No, not in this goddamn heat. He shrugs and crosses to the coffee shop.

He has just come on duty and it's going to be a long eight hours. Quiet, he thinks. Uneventful, he thinks, though later tonight, astonished and sick at the incredible sight, it will be he who files the report and summons the ambulance for the five bodies.

Mrs. Fayer has reached an intersection and looks both ways. She is forcing herself not to think of Martha, of Adam, of that insane Mercedes. She knows what they do with it and she knows about the boys they pick up and she knows why.

"What does that have to do with me?" she says, not knowing. "They have nothing to do with me."

The hill is steeper now and, despite the shade trees, the heat is even more unbearable. Mrs. Fayer leans against an iron fence with spikes at the top. Beyond the fence there is a garden and a courtyard of flagstones. She can hear water playing in a fountain. She wants to rest. She wants to stop.

Surely at her age it is possible to stop. To sit down in a rocking chair—by a fire if it's winter or by a mint julep if it's summer—and kick off the shoes, and put the old feet up on a hassock. Just stop. Live in the past a little, live in memory. Surely at her age there are plenty of memories.

But Mrs. Fayer is trapped in the present tense. She has no past, in the sense of things that have happened. Whatever has happened is happening to her now. And so she listens to the water playing in the fountain and thinks about finding them, the two women.

Then, for no reason, she turns abruptly and faces the two young men who are about to cross the street. They stop as they see her staring, step back onto the sidewalk, and continue up the hill. At the next corner, they separate. With her fist Mrs. Fayer smooths the pain beneath her ribs. Purse snatchers, and she an old woman, defenseless. She laughs, softly.

"Mrs. Price," she says.

"Lulu Mercer," she says.

She will go to Louisburg Square and sit. There is a green bench in the little garden. She will find the women later. And who can tell, perhaps they too are sitting in Louisburg Square.

Perhaps she is not supposed to find the women. And yet she is sure she is. It will happen yet, she knows, that blinding flash, that revelation. She sets out to meet it.

And so Mrs. Fayer is in Louisburg Square. She pauses at the iron lamppost when she sees the young man coming toward her. He is striding with a purpose, not looking at her, looking straight ahead as if she were not there. He is alone. Where is his partner? She throws a quick glance around the tiny square; there is no one to call out to for help. There never is.

Perhaps he will only take her pocketbook, not strike her, not throw her to the ground and . . . Perhaps he has a knife and will use it. Perhaps he is insane. She imagines the blade slipping between her ribs and then she feels it twist. But this is absurd. Things like this don't happen in midafternoon, in the blinding sun, in the middle of Louisburg Square. But they do, and Mrs. Fayer knows it.

So this is the moment for which she has lived her entire life? No, it makes no sense. One hand on the iron lamppost, she braces her feet for the attack.

"Mrs. Price," she says, trying to call for help.

"Lulu . . ."

She does not finish Lulu Mercer's name because, though the young man is still three feet away from her, a fist plunges into her back and sends her sprawling on the pavement. Her pocketbook flies from her hand and spins around twice in the air before it crashes to the ground, open. The second young man springs from behind her and snatches at the pocketbook. He tips everything onto the cobblestone street.

Together the two young men rummage through the bunch of letters, notes, junk of all kinds. They find the wallet. The wallet is fat, but it contains mostly yellowed photographs and a few pictures of saints with prayers on the back. There are several charge plates, an American Express card. They pocket these. They are in a hurry now. They have no time. Anybody might come along. The police. Adam. Anybody. They tear the pictures and the holy cards in half and continue searching. In the zippered section of the wallet they discover twenty-two dollars and some change. A good hit. They look around and of course the coast is clear. They walk slowly down the hill for a block or so, and then as they near Charles Street they begin to run, laughing, punching one another.

And Mrs. Fayer lies on the sidewalk in Louisburg Square, her body shaded by an ancient oak tree, only her head exposed to the light.

Her breath comes in gasps. She is unconscious and one hand has begun to bleed where it was skinned on the cobblestones. And though she is unconscious, she sees a blinding light before her eyes and hears a voice from somewhere deep beneath the pain and the labored breathing, a voice that laughs as it says, "But I'm alive. I am alive."

Mrs. Fayer is in the present, in Boston, on a sweltering September afternoon in the year 1976.

2

Mrs. Fayer is in the present, in Amherst, on a mild July morning in the year 1970. She is frying eggs for Mrs. Price's breakfast. This is not the present she would prefer to be in—as she lies on the sidewalk in Louisburg Square—but we make our choices and we must live with them.

So Mrs. Fayer is seventy now, being born in 1900, and she is fed up. She tastes iron filings beneath her tongue and at odd times, though she cannot imagine why, all her teeth ache. Sometimes she gets a burning pain in one eye, quick and terrible, as if someone were probing there with a needle. She walks more slowly than before. And she must have tea in the middle of the morning just to get through till noon. This is all part of being seventy, she knows, but she is fed up with it just the same. And so she has sold the Hillside Rest Home to the Harrows, outright. She is done with it, she is done with all of them.

"This is the last egg I will ever fry in my life," Mrs. Fayer says, and she raps the shell smartly against the pan. The egg plops into the steaming butter and then, for no reason she can see, the yolk breaks.

"Oh, God damn." She cracks a second egg and settles it perfectly into the pan. So much for Mrs. Price's eggs, one sunny-side and one collapsed.

She moves over to the sink and leans against it, looking out the window. There is nothing to see except the gravel driveway and the bed of phlox and zinnias; the barn that used to stand there has been pulled down.

Almost at once she hears the sound of tires on the gravel and a minute later a battered Chevy lurches to a halt inches from the bed of flowers. The car door flies open and a girl's legs, long and bare and black, appear from behind it. And then the girl herself, cool in a deep green minidress. She plunges back into the car and drags out the red leather hatbox she carries everywhere. Slamming the car door with her foot, she adjusts the bag on her shoulder and with her free hand gives Mrs. Fayer a huge wave. And then she walks up the flagstone path to the house. Martha has arrived for work.

Mrs. Fayer, shaking her head, returns to the eggs. She has never accustomed herself to Martha's walk; those sinuous thighs and the gently bobbing breasts and above all the tilted head on that long neck make only one response possible. "She'll get arrested," Mrs. Fayer said the first time she saw her walk, and she has not changed her opinion since. The kitchen door bangs open.

"Mawnin, Miz Fayer. How y'all feelin dis fine mawnin?" Martha is in high spirits and is Uncle Tomming it.

"Mawin yourself. You're early today."

"Mmmm. Cinnamon toast, my favorite," she says, shaking crumbs into the sink. "That's because I thought you might need some extra help this morning."

"Well, that's plumb sweet of you, honey, but no, I think everything's under control. The Harrows should be here before noon and you can do the lunches, but I won't need you for a while."

"We're gonna miss you, you cute old thing." Martha brushes crumbs from her mouth with the tip of one long finger and kisses Mrs. Fayer loudly on the cheek. "We will." She swings about so that her breasts shake beneath the green dress. "Gotta change," she says. "It'll take me a while in the john, it's that time."

Mrs. Fayer does not answer. She is thinking that someone is going to miss her. Someone says they are going to miss her. Martha. Martha has a husband and a child, a young boy.

She has a mother-in-law who looks after the boy while Martha is working. She is a door slammer and a dish banger. But she is lively and the old people like her, all of them, even Butley who is from Georgia and who says that the only good Nigra is a dead Nigra. Mrs. Fayer chews on her lower lip. No, they will not miss her. They might miss Martha if she were to leave, but they will not miss her.

"Take your time," she says to Martha, but Martha has already left the kitchen and is going now through the back passage that is used as a storeroom. She goes up the steep narrow stairs to the attic above the garage, her red bag rattling on the bannister. She passes the bathroom door and throws open the door next to it.

"Okay, whitey," she says, "you've been asking for it and now you're going to get it, but good."

Adam Brockway twists his head on the pillow and makes a face at her. "Snack time," he says. "Bring it over here."

Martha takes a few steps into the room and leans one elbow on the old bureau. "Come and get it," she says.

He lies in bed watching for a change of expression on her face.

She stands leaning against the bureau, studying his impossibly skinny body beneath the sheet.

A minute passes. He snaps his fingers at her and she turns her head away. He laughs then and immediately she laughs too and comes and stands by the bed. He runs his hand up her thigh and then back and forth between her legs, gently pressing the hard sleek flesh.

"Christ, don't you ever wear underpants?"

"They're in the bag. I'll put them on after."

Lazily, he kicks the sheet off and watches her eyes travel up and down his long white body. This is the part he likes best, lying there watching her want him. She reaches down to touch him but he will not let her, not yet.

"God, you're so skinny," she says. "How did you ever get so skinny?"

"I worked for it. Dropping acid does it."

"I love it," she says. "I love it right here where . . ."

"Shh," he says. "Don't talk. It's better when you don't talk.

"When are you gonna let *me* drop acid?"

"Shh," he says. "Not now."

He continues to stroke the inside of her thighs, slipping his hand through to the strong small buttocks, and then back and forth, probing.

Adam is twenty-one and has been a sophisticate of sex since he dropped out of Choate at sixteen. Only the variations interest him now. Some day he is going to write about all this in a way it's never been done before. He is going to be a famous novelist, like Henry Miller, only better. Right now he is gathering material. When he is twenty-five, when he gets his money, then he'll have the time to write it. Until then, he is the handyman at Hillside. Real handy, he thinks, and presses harder on her slick clitoris.

But Martha can stand it no longer. She reaches behind her for the zipper of her dress.

"Okay, let's start," he says, less interested already.

Downstairs, Mrs. Fayer has not gone on with serving breakfast after all. She has remained standing at the window, her mind numb as she stares at the phlox and zinnias.

"Phlox and zinnias," she says, and casts an eye toward the frying pan where the eggs have begun to curl at the edges. She is completely absorbed in the browning eggs and yet suddenly she gets the feeling that someone is watching her.

She turns in time to see Mrs. Price back away from the door, a smile playing at her lips. Mrs. Price is crazy, or almost, but that makes no difference to Mrs. Fayer at the moment; she does not like people staring at her when she doesn't know they're there. She pokes the one golden yoke with her spatula; now both yokes are broken.

"Good," she says. "There's too much staring going on in this world anyhow."

As she talks to herself, aloud, she slides the eggs smoothly on to a heated plate and the plate on to the tray. She adds two slices of cinnamon toast, orange juice, coffee, and then she takes the tray down the corridor to Mrs. Price's room. The door is ajar, but she knocks anyway, balancing the tray on the palm of her hand. Mrs. Price is dressed and sitting in her chair.

"You're up and around early this morning," Mrs. Fayer says her voice not quite accusatory, but not friendly either.

"I'm dying."

"That's all right."

Mrs. Fayer places a board across the arms of the chair and sets the tray down on it. She arranges the plates and the silverware for Mrs. Price's convenience. It is all part of a ritual the sick woman has come to expect.

"I'm dying," she says again, tonelessly as always.

"That's all right. We're all dying."

Mrs. Fayer steps back and looks at Mrs. Price who only stares at her with large dull eyes.

"I'm dying."

"Well, you just eat now and postpone dying for a while." Mrs. Fayer leaves to collect the breakfast trays she has finally finished handing out.

Though Hillside is nominally a rest home, Mrs. Price is the one resident who is actually recovering from anything. The eight others are merely old. They think that Mrs. Price is not all right in the head because, during the past two years, she has said nothing except "I'm dying," whereas they have no interest in dying and do not like to hear it mentioned.

Mrs. Fayer does not mind her. She is easy to care for, certainly easier than the eight others, and since she does not speak, she demands a minimum of conversation from Mrs. Fayer, who is tired of talking anyway. Besides, she has obligations to Jessie Price.

Many, many years back, when Mrs. Fayer was still Sister

Judith, her friend Ruth Price had come to visit her at St. Vincent's, and had brought her daughter Jessie. They had talked, nervous and tense, and then Ruth Price had suddenly said, "Promise me. You must promise me, Judith." And Sister Judith nodded and said, "Of course." Ruth Price smiled then. "If anything happens to me," she said, "you'll take her. You have to now, you've promised." And so the child Jessie Price came to St. Vincent's home for children at the age of eight, motherless, and fell in love with Sister Judith. But then Sister Judith left the convent and became Mrs. Fayer and Jessie Price disappeared from her life forever, almost.

And so Mrs. Fayer has a kind of obligation to Jessie Price. She has other obligations to her—perhaps—but she refuses to think of them.

Jesse Price—but everyone calls her Mrs. Price—has been at Hillside for over two years, and she has not improved. She will never improve. She sits silent and staring, coiled into herself like a sybil. "I'm dying," she says, only that.

Mrs. Fayer has no special affection for her, not after all that has passed between them. She has no special affection for any of the old people; rather, a general benevolence toward the nine. They are living proof of a job well done. And the job *is* done. She is leaving it today.

If there is a God, he is looking down on her and saying, well done.

The telephone rings sharply, but only once. She waits for a second ring that does not come. She holds her breath and her pulse beats faster, harder. She waits. Finally she leaves the kitchen to collect the breakfast trays and immediately the phone begins to ring again. It keeps on ringing. Why should she panic because a telephone is ringing?

Mrs. Fayer has read many books and she has seen television nightly and she knows that anything might happen when she picks up the receiver. There could be silence on the other end and, after a moment, the harsh breathing of a crazy man or a sex maniac. Or there could be simply a voice saying, "You are being watched," and then a click as the receiver is put down, leaving her to figure out if this is a joke or if someone is trying to drive her mad. Or there could be a threat, "Some night when you are sleeping, I will set fire to the house." This is 1970 and these things happen, she knows.

She waits for one more ring and then, jaw clenched, she lifts the receiver. From the other end a calm voice, a normal voice, says to her, "My name is Lulu Mercer and I'm trying to get in touch with a party named Connolly? I wonder if you could help me?"

But Mrs. Fayer is still thinking of the sex maniac and the arsonist and, distracted, says that there is no Connolly at the Hillside Rest Home.

Only when the caller has hung up does it occur to her that her own name is Connolly, that perhaps the voice, calm and normal, had some message for her. She puts the receiver down hard.

"Connolly," she says.

How long is it since she has thought of herself as Jessica Connolly? She is Mrs. Fayer and that is the end of it.

"Get on with it," she says, and does.

• • •

Mrs. Fayer is lying on the cobblestone sidewalk in Louisburg Square. There is no traffic in the Square, or at least no one has stopped to see if she is injured. She lies there for a long time. Finally the sunlight playing on her face makes her sneeze and she comes conscious.

A man with a walking stick is sauntering down the hill. He twirls the stick, he taps the gold-green leaves that hang above him. And then he sees Mrs. Fayer lying on the sidewalk. He stops long enough to see she is trying to sit up, and he moves ahead to help her. But then he notices her pocketbook open and the contents spilled in the gutter and he realizes what must have happened. He crosses the street quickly and, at a little distance, begins to whistle. He knows the dangers of getting involved.

Mrs. Fayer sits on the sidewalk, her back against the iron lamppost. She sees her photographs and holy cards lying in halves in the street. She can make out the forehead and eyes of Dr. Turner, the lips and heavy jaw of her husband Eugene. A few letters are scattered about and her little gold compact lies open, the mirror crushed by a foot. She moves her hand toward the nearest photograph but she cannot reach it. She rests her head against the iron post.

She smiles.

• • •

Mrs. Fayer is back in the present, in 1970, and there is work to be done. "Get on with it," she says, and she does.

She goes to the farthest room and the room next to it, collecting the breakfast trays, scattering to the beds and chairs the same cheerful remarks she has scattered morning after morning for the past forty years.

"Ah, you look lovely with your hair all combed up."

"You've not finished your toast, but you did lovely on your eggs."

"You must sit by the window; the morning sun is lovely."

She does not think of the walled garden in the convent orphanage. She does not think of herself at Nones, the white veil falling forward as she bends in prayer. Sister Judith. She thinks of the brightly colored plastic trays she must pick up and clean off and place upright in the dishwasher. "The morning sun is lovely," she says and takes the first two trays down the stairs and along the corridor and into the sunlit kitchen.

This is her last breakfast at Hillside and she is glad. She is done with it. She is done with all of them. In a way, old Butley is responsible for her going. It was his casual, malicious remark that made her realize the emptiness of her life and made her decide to do something about it.

Coming back from Dr. Turner's funeral, distracted and

in tears, she was met by Butley on the front steps. He had been waiting for her. "Well, Henry Turner's gone now," he said. "Guess there's nothing too much left for you." And as she stared at him, astonished, Butley added, "It's anybody's bet who'll be next. Us . . . or you." And then he cackled, delighted with himself. This was in February and by March Mrs. Fayer had put Hillside up for sale. She would show old Butley. She would show them all. She would live.

It is July now. Dr. Turner has been dead five months and Mrs. Fayer is leaving Hillside for good. She will live for herself. For the first time ever, she is free: no convent superiors, no accusing husband, no more constant smell of death and dying. She is free. By late afternoon she will be in an apartment on Marlborough Street. She will start a new life. They are done with, all the people who have used her and abused her and driven her back into her self for survival. And Dr. Turner, lost.

If only she had married him. He had asked her, had wanted to leave Louise, had even told her he was leaving her, but then Louise had taken the pills, slashed her wrists, and was found half-dead in the bathtub. And where had Dr. Turner been? At the home of Jessica Fayer, planning a new life with her. And so Louise had won. She kept her Henry, as she called him, but she became more and more peculiar. There was some woman, some tramp, she said, who was after her money. There was a plot against her, but she was keeping notes, she was writing it all down. In the end, she was completely mad, but harmless. Before he died, Dr. Turner committed her to a private mental home. And he himself, lost.

"I'll live," Mrs. Fayer says aloud, and surveys the room, satisfied she is leaving behind her a kitchen that can be faulted in every respect except cleanliness.

Upstairs, in the room above the garage, Adam and Martha fall away from each other, exhausted by their calisthenics. He lies on his back panting. She continues to play with him, using her tongue, nipping him with her teeth. She is exhausted too, but she continues, knowing he is still not satisfied.

"Try something new," he says, "think of something we've never done before."

She drops him then and wipes her sticky hand on the sheet.

"Up yours, whitey," she says.

He thinks about what she has said. "We haven't tried that," he says, and he raises his eyebrows, only half joking.

Mrs. Fayer goes from room to room collecting the breakfast trays and washing them, washing the dishes and pans she has cooked in.

"I am washing the dishes now. I am washing the pans." She speaks to herself, aloud, telling herself what she is doing. It is an old habit, begun when Eugene ran off, and continued during the thirty-five years that have followed. "I am stacking the trays now on the metal table by the door."

It is a way of keeping sane. Besides, there is nothing to feel one way or another about stacking trays and dishes. It is something you can talk about.

She is giddy with not thinking. She wants to lie down. The pain in her chest has slipped and is lodged beneath her ribs now. Something must happen. Something has got to break this moment, end it, or she will stand forever looking at this kitchen, not thinking, while the pain grows and swells in her chest.

"I have survived them all," she says, and the telephone rings.

"Mrs. Fayer? Is this Mrs. Fayer?" The voice cracks and splinters, there are sobs and small choking sounds. It is Emma Lee Washington, in tears because her son Bill is in the hospital in critical condition. He has fallen from a scaffolding. Martha should know. Can Mrs. Fayer tell her? Right away? Of course. Of course.

More death. More dying. Mrs. Fayer moves slowly through the storage hall to the foot of the stairs. In her mind she sees a black man lying in a tangle of white sheets. She touches him, and he is not Bill Washington. She stops at the stairs and forces herself back into the present.

Mrs. Washington called and says you should go home right away; it's about Bill. Mrs. Fayer says this to herself and then she repeats it twice so she will get it right.

Her foot is on the first stair when suddenly the door to Adam's room flies open and Martha runs out, laughing, looking back. She poses on the landing, one hand behind her tugging the zipper up. She is laughing loudly, a high taunting laugh, and Adam, laughing too, runs out on the stairs after her. He lunges at the zipper, trying to pull it down. As they struggle together, laughing and grabbing, he finally notices Mrs. Fayer.

One hand rests on the bannister, the other is at her heart. Her foot is lifted in the act of climbing a stair. She gazes at them, not angry, only astounded—at Martha, half out of her green dress and at Adam, his chalk white body completely naked. For a full minute the couple at the head of the stairs looks down and Mrs. Fayer looks back at them.

"Your mother called and you have to go home right away. Your mother-in-law. It's about Bill."

Martha stares at Mrs. Fayer for a moment, confused, and then she reaches behind her for the zipper. Adam helps her slide the zipper up. She tugs at the hem of her dress.

"It's about Bill, she said. She said it's serious and you should come home." Mrs. Fayer is reciting from memory. She is being tactful, but there is no need for tact: they all know that Martha's husband will die. That is how things happen.

"I'll get my bag," Martha says.

"I'll get it," Adam says, and disappears into the little room. He hands her the bag and then, stepping back, pulls a towel from inside the door and wraps it around his waist.

Martha comes down the stairs, her bag clattering on the bannister rails, and disappears through the hallway.

Mrs. Fayer continues to stand at the foot of the stairs, one hand at her heart. "Virgil," she says, and lifts her hand to her forehead. Outside there is the roar of a motor and the sound of car wheels on the gravel as Martha drives away. Mrs. Fayer waves her hand before her eyes, brushing away something invisible. "You can help me give out the lunches," she says finally. "You'll have to help with the lunch trays."

"Sure," Adam says. "Okay."

"I'll be in my room lying down for the next hour," she says, and as she turns to go she sees him staring after her, his towel bunched at his protruding hipbone. He is grinning.

In the storage hall, she stops to get her bearings. The room is stuffy, airless. Cases of soap and toilet paper and canned goods line the walls, and in the center there are crates of linen, making the room merely a passageway. Mrs. Fayer leans against the windowsill and looks out at nothing. She is not going to think of it, not any of it. Not Bill Washington falling from a scaffolding, not that tangle of black and white flesh at the head of the stairs, and not Virgil Clark either. Especially not Virgil Clark.

Mrs. Fayer concentrates on the housefly buzzing at the window. A soothing sound; it is summer; nothing terrible can happen. And then, gradually, she becomes aware of another sound in the room. The sound of breathing.

She lets her eyes wander over as much of the room as she can see without moving. Mrs. Price is standing in the corner, staring at her with those gray empty eyes.

Mrs. Fayer makes a startled sound just as Mrs. Price says something, and so she misses what it was.

Has she said, as always, "I'm dying," or has she said "You're dying"; which?

The fly buzzes at the window, trying to get out.

"What? What did you say?"

She listens for an answer but there is none. Mrs. Price only stares, one side of her mouth twisted in pain or amusement. The room is filled with the fly's furious buzzing.

3

Sister Judith is in the present tense, but it is not clear when. She is young; she is still many years away from becoming Mrs. Fayer.

She is in a hospital. The walls are pale green, eye-ease, and the floors are black and white tile. Is she a patient? Is she a nurse? There is no time to tell.

She has rushed from the operating room, about to be sick, and now she leans her forehead against the cool green wall, waiting for the nausea to pass. In a moment she feels the blood pulsing in her brow and knows she will be all right.

She steps into the first room to her right and falls into the bedside chair. She had wanted to be a nurse, but none of this was what she expected. She has never dodged into rooms, never fallen into chairs. She looks up and sees a young man looking back at her.

He is not in bed. He is in a wheelchair and his face is horribly disfigured. Part of his cheek has been shot away, one eye gone with it, and most of his nose and his upper lip. He is staring at her and she cannot help staring back at him.

His face twists, what is left of it, as he tries to smile. He has hair the color of sand and his remaining eye is deep blue, almost purple. He smiles once more.

"I'm not really like this," he says, the words bubbling in his crooked mouth. He manages some deprecating gesture. What is it? A shrug of his shoulder? Does he tip his head slightly?

She sees him.

"No. No, you're not," she says, and pushes herself from her chair. She kneels at his feet and gently slips her arms around his waist, lowering her head to kiss his chest. She can feel the soft brown hairs beneath the cotton nightgown. She raises her head, kissing his neck, letting her saliva run along his collar bone. Below, she can feel him begin to stiffen. She moves her mouth to his ear and then to his chin. She touches it with her tongue. He is breathing deeply, abandoning himself.

"No, you're not like this," she says, and presses her wet mouth against his broken one. Her tongue slides on his teeth. Their breath is thick between them. It expands. It takes up all the space inside them both. They are welded to each other like this forever. They will die this way.

"Gordon?" she says. "Who?"

This is a dream, a nightmare. If she can just hold on, if she can just remember who she is, it will all pass, it will be over.

She pulls away from him for a second and looks him in the face, but it is no longer the ruined face of a stranger, it is her own face she sees.

Surrender, she thinks. Surrender. This time it will be easy to accept.

But she knows she does not, because later she remembers someone carrying her from the room.

4

Jessica is feeding a sheet through the wringer with her left hand as she turns the crank with her right. A shaft of sunlight comes through the cellar window and falls in a jagged pattern on the square of linoleum that marks off the laundry area. She stares at the light for a moment and then squints hard to relieve the stinging in her eyes. The air around her is hot and wet, suffocating, and the smell of lye makes her head ache. But she is not going to be sick, she cannot. She leans against the machine to steady herself and the moment passes.

The sheet trails through the wringer finally and plops into the rinse tub. Jessica plunges her arms deep into the soapy water and feels around for any last bit of laundry. She comes up with a handkerchief, a tiny square of white linen embroidered in one corner with three red strawberries. Whose?

Jessica is a plain woman of thirty-three, her red hair going brown already. She is thin and clothes hang on her in a way that exaggerates her thinness. And she is tall. Walking, even sitting, she seems to pull into herself, as if she were trying to pass unnoticed. Her mouth is small, but her lips are perfectly formed. Her nose, broken once and then badly set, has a bump on it, and the bridge is too broad for the slender nostrils. But it is her eyes that people remember. Large and widely spaced, they are a deep green with tiny flecks of gold on the outer edges of the iris. A cat's eyes, but with a warmth that is compelling.

It is a raw spring day in the year 1933. Jessica has been married for three years to Eugene Henderson Fayer and for three years, too, she has done the laundry and the cooking and the nursing for the four old ladies at Hillside. She has done the work willingly, eagerly even, as a distraction from her marriage, which is unhappy, which is disastrous. And now she is pregnant.

Satisfied that everything is in the rinse tub, Jessica unhooks the hose and empties the soapy water into the metal drain in the center of the floor. She stands looking into the tub as the water level goes down, leaving little rings of soap on the edges. She is thinking something hard, something desperate, as she stands there gripping the rim of the washing machine.

The soapy water gurgles from the hose into the drain and Jessica listens to it. She does not hear Virgil Clark open the door to the cellar nor does she hear his feet on the stairs. He has come to carry the basket of wet laundry out to the clotheslines. He stands at a little distance waiting to be noticed.

Another wave of nausea comes over her and she presses the heel of her palm against her mouth. After a minute it passes and she looks up into the somber black face of Virgil Clark.

"It's too hot and close down here," he says.

"It's got to be done." She smiles at him.

"It's too much for you."

He waits, trying to catch her glance, but she says nothing and so he picks up the large wicker basket of laundry and moves toward the door. Almost at once he hears a high sharp cry behind him and turns in time to see Jessica bend in two, her hands clasped to her stomach, her head thrown back. For a minute or more she crouches like that, consumed by the pain, while Virgil puts down the laundry basket and bends down beside her, helpless. She stands finally and looks straight into his eyes. She is not searching for any response;

she trusts him. She places her hands on his shoulders and lowers her head to his chest.

"Oh God," she says, "what am I going to do?"

Virgil can smell the stale gin on her breath. She is crying now and her body shakes as she pulls herself closer to him. Virgil casts a glance at the cellar window; nobody outside could see through it unless they got on their knees. He looks up the stairs to the kitchen and then at the hatchway that gives on to the backyard. Eugene was limping down toward the chicken coop when Virgil last saw him. So they are alone, they are safe. He could take this woman right here on the linoleum, toss her around on the soaking laundry. This is what she wants, whether or not she knows it. He wonders how much she does know. When she realizes what it is she wants, she will come to him for it. He will not take her now. It is 1933 and he is black, and so he waits.

"I'm sorry," she says at last, pulling away from him. "I'm sorry, Virgil, I'm not myself. I'm . . ." Her voice trails off and she smooths her eyes with a handkerchief that she takes from inside her dress. "Why don't you . . ." and, still running the handkerchief beneath her eyes, she points to the basket of sheets.

Virgil only stands where he is, looking at her.

Their eyes meet and for a second she seems to realize what is in his mind, or perhaps what is in her own mind, and she bites her lower lip, shaking her head sideways as she does so.

"The laundry," she says, and gestures vaguely toward the basket and then toward the hatchway. Virgil's shirt has dark patches from the water, where her hands were on his shoulders. And there is another spot, smaller, on his chest, this one made by her tears.

They stand this way, looking at each other, caught in a present that can never change, the light forever playing on the floor between them in a crazy zigzag pattern. She is plain, but with eyes that are warm and green and full of tenderness. He is black and compactly built, with a body that must be lithe and powerful beneath the shabby work clothes he wears. They can take one step forward and make their lives, in that single act, different from what they are, what they will be. Or they can stand this way, looking at each other, forever. And they do.

At once, the light on the floor is shattered and Eugene stands in the door of the hatchway, looking from his wife to his hired hand and back again.

Jessica, released, moves to the washing machine and Virgil Clark bends to the wicker basket full of laundry.

Eugene Fayer slams the hatchway door as Virgil disappears with the laundry. He is waiting for her to say something, anything, but she only loads the washer with the last batch of linens and says nothing to him. He leans against the door and coughs. He is wearing the green overcoat of an army captain, which still fits him fifteen years after the war. His chin juts out aggressively and his full lips are pulled back in anger. He runs a hand over his hair, which is gray and thick, and he coughs again. He was gassed in the war and then shot and left for dead, but somehow he recovered. Now he limps when he walks and his bleeding lungs have left him with a cough, strained and gasping, whenever he is angry. And he is angry now.

"I'm slow," he says. "I'm so goddamned slow."

She adds the soap and pokes at the linens with her washing stick.

"I didn't figure it out until today. I was on my way down to the chicken coop when it hit me. Like a revelation, as *you* would say," and he fills the word *you* with scorn. "All of a sudden I understood what the hell's been going on with you for the past month. Singing that goddamn "Ave Maria" all the time. Oh yes, I heard you," he says, but she will not answer. "I heard you singing all the old convent numbers, and I figured you were just wishing for the good old days." He coughs and wipes his lips with the back of his hand. When he begins again his voice is higher, thinner. "And then there was the forgetfulness; all of a sudden you can't remember where you put anything or what you said ten minutes ago. And your looks too, your looks should have been a giveaway, you've been looking like hell, but I missed that too. And then it hit me all of a sudden as I was going down to the chickens. You're a drunk, is what. You've been hitting the old gin bottle." He comes toward her, not limping now. "How often do you do it, huh? A big nip at breakfast and supper? Or do you spread it out over the whole day, a little before breakfast, a little after breakfast, a sip with the old ladies, a sip with the nigger. How do you do it?"

At last she looks at him. "I haven't been drinking gin."

"Goddamn you, don't lie to me. I know fucking well you've been drinking it and I know how much. You had some this morning, for Christ's sake!"

"Liar!"

He is satisfied now that he has pushed her into anger, so his own anger subsides. He smiles.

"I've never lied to you. You knew from the beginning what you were getting when you married me; an army captain with bad lungs and a bad leg and big prick. I'm the one that didn't know. I married a nun and it turns out I get a drunk. Nice. That's really nice, Sister Judith."

Jessica leans against the washing machine waiting for it to end. She is not going to cry. She is not going to get sick.

"What do you want, Eugene? In the name of God, what exactly do you want?"

"What do I want? You make me laugh, you know that? You lean over the goddamn washer like some suffering saint and you say to me, what do you want. Look at you. Jesus, you make me sick."

Jessica is running fresh water in the rinse tub. She pokes the soapy linens as they chug back and forth in the washing machine. She is busy. Let him rave.

"Do you know what you are? You're thirty-three years old

and you look fifty. You're dried up. You're dead. You should never have left that convent, you know that? That's where you belong—locked up with a bunch of dried up old maids. Except you wouldn't like it there now, I guess. They don't provide you with gin in the convent."

She looks at him with hatred.

"How long has this been going on anyway? Hmmm? Oh, I know it's been going on for a while. I notice there's been a peculiar amount of miscellaneous on the medicine bills. What exactly do you call miscellaneous? Which one of the old girls is using all the miscellaneous?"

"If you want me to list every single bit of cotton gauze and Mercurochrome and Vaseline separately, and put the women's names next to it, then I will. Now will you please leave me alone."

"Oh, I'll leave you alone all right. I just want to know one thing. Are you telling me that you haven't been buying extra gin and putting it down in the accounts as something else? That's all I want to know, Jessica. It's a very reasonable question."

"I'm telling you nothing."

"Because you see, Jessica, all I have to do is ask old Dietel how much gin you've been buying, and he'll not only tell me, he'll be real interested to know why I want to know."

"You do that, you just go ahead and do that."

He sneers at her across the laundry tub.

"Drunk!"

She waits, staring him down, but this time his eyes do not fall. She is frantic now, all motion. She moves around the washing machine so that her back is to him. She does not have to see him. But he stalks her, pacing in a circle, thrusting his head in toward her so that he is constantly in her way.

"Do you know something?" he says. "Do you know what you are?"

But she is not listening. Her hand closes on the washing

stick and she stabs at the soapy linens, plunging the stick wildly into the churning water. "Leave me alone," she shouts, as her hand slashes at the linens and the water spills out, slapping the linoleum floor.

"Listen to me," he shouts. "Goddamn you, listen to me."

He grabs her by the shoulder and spins her around to face him. "Do you want to know?" he is saying, but she does not hear. She is screaming. She hurls the stick across the cellar and, still screaming, runs for the stairs. But he catches her and with his two hands pins her against the massive brick column that supports the main beam of the house. She cannot move. She does not even try. She is exhausted.

He holds her with her arms pinned against the bricks until her chest stops heaving and her breath comes more normally again. Her head is tilted to one side and a heavy strand of hair has come loose and hangs over her face.

"I'm pregnant," she says, her voice dead.

He loosens his hold on her, but slowly. This could be one of her tricks.

"I am," she says.

He has told her there will be no children, and he uses a prophylactic so that she has no choice.

They are in the present now, in 1933, as he steps away from her, looking, but they are in the present of 1930 as well. They are newly married. She has not yet had time to think of herself as Jessica Fayer; she is still, in her mind, Sister Judith. She has been out of the convent less than a week and she is married to Eugene Henderson Fayer—without the blessing of the Church she has served for thirty years. He needs her, this cold crippled man, and she has married him. She waits, staring at the ceiling, while he smooths the rubber tube free of wrinkles. And then he is plunging at her, saying something, "Come on, give, goddamn it," and he pries her open. She is conspiring in her own rape. She tries. She is watching shadows move against the ceiling. And then he is done. He rolls over, his back to her, and sleeps. Jessica lies for a long while listening to him breathe. She matches the rhythm of her own breath to his. So this is sex. So this is love. She does not close her eyes and sleep; she stares straight ahead, taking a long and joyless look at what she has done. We make our choices, she knows, and then they make us.

This present is always with her and it is with her now, in 1933, as she stands facing Eugene. She rubs her elbows which have been scraped by the rough bricks, and then she pushes back the loose strand of hair and pins it.

"You can't be," he says, and adds in a different voice, "pregnant."

"I am."

"Well, you're not having it. I'll get a doctor."

As he goes up the stairs, coughing, he turns back and says, "Whose is it anyway, that nigger's?"

In the middle of the afternoon he leaves his hoeing and goes to look for her. She is where she always is at this time, in the kitchen; she is making the pea soup for the evening's supper.

"Do you realize we haven't got any money? Do you realize we may be out of business tomorrow, waiting in bread lines, and you want to have a baby?"

"I'm having the baby."

"A nigger bastard, that's what it is."

"It's our baby, yours and mine, and I'm having it."

At night, lying side by side in their marriage bed, he says to her, "Jessica, you've got to be reasonable. I need you, you know that. You've got to go to the doctor."

"No doctor would . . ."

"But in Boston, maybe even in Springfield . . ."

"I'm having the baby."

"Jessica." He places his hand on her, just beneath her breasts, and begins to move it upward. Jessica tears back the covers and springs out of bed. In one motion, in the dark, she snatches at her felt slippers and her woolen robe and is at the door. But he makes no move to follow her.

"Yes, go and drink your goddamn gin," he says.

She is outside the room, her slippers and her robe clutched against her chest, when she hears him shout at the closed door, "And then go and fuck your nigger."

• • •

Jessica drinks gin. The year is 1933 and she cannot legally purchase the gin she has only begun, now, to drink. And so she purchases it for medicinal purposes at Dietel's Pharmacy. No one questions her. No one wonders. Everyone knows about Eugene, and if his wife drinks, it is because she has been given plenty of reasons.

Jessica has begun drinking only during the past month. She missed her period for the second time and knew for certain what she had already suspected; she was pregnant. With Eugene's child. He would be enraged, she knew; she could see him storming through the kitchen in his first fury, and then as the rage deepened, he would grow silent and just stand there, watching as she worked, waiting for the poisonous word to come to him, to attack, to crush. She could not edure it, not even the thought of it. Then, as if she had no control whatsoever over her own actions, she drifted slowly, meditatively, to the medicine closet, unlocked it, and stood there watching her hand close around the neck of the bottle, watching as the hand poured the gin into the tumbler, watching until the clear acid liquid was at her lips. She blinked at the sharp smell of the gin and then, watching no longer but doing it, she poured the liquid into her mouth. In two huge gulps she emptied the glass. That was the beginning.

And now she has been drinking for almost a month, but only a little at a time, enough to deaden the present she cannot live in.

• • •

At the foot of the stairs Jessica puts on her robe and slippers. The house is freezing and she hugs herself as she wanders from room to room. The four old women are asleep, the sound of snoring filters down the corridor. Jessica stands at the window of the darkened parlor and looks out at the road and the steep hill and the meadow. She saw three deer in that meadow, a buck and two young does, only last winter. Last winter, when she was not expecting a child, when her only misery was knowing that she was not loved, that she never had been loved. The deer have never returned, of course.

"Love," she says aloud, her voice bitter.

And now she is pregnant with a child she desperately wants. But how is it possible to raise a child whose father hates it? And hates the mother?

Eugene is lying in the bed upstairs, waiting. Jessica has come to know him well, she knows the pattern and the rhythms of his cruelty, just as he will come to know the patterns and rhythms of her drunkenness.

Eugene is waiting, but Jessica cannot know what he is waiting for.

Numb, she turns from the black window and drifts along the corridor, past the old women sleeping, past the stairwell and the dining room, and into—as she must—the kitchen. Her face is expressionless and there is a glassy look to her eyes. She has trouble fitting the key into the lock of the medicine closet. It is as if she is already drunk; the empty gaze, the vagueness of her movements, the sleepy walk. She opens the door and, without even looking, finds the bottle with her hand and takes it to the sink. The tumbler is half filled when she realizes she is being watched. She turns slowly. Eugene is standing in the doorway, grinning as if he were happy.

"Oh, Sister Judith," he says, and goes away, limping.

Jessica drinks the scalding liquor with her eyes closed and then she half fills the glass once more. The bottle dangles from her limp hand as she wanders back along the corridor to the darkened parlor, sipping at the gin as she goes. "Sister Judith," she says, but already the words mean nothing to her.

She goes to the window and stands looking across the road

to the steep hill and the meadow. The gin is working and time stops for her. The deer have never come back. There is only this cold spring night and the moonlight golden on the meadow grass, and nothing, nothing is alive.

How long does she stand there? And why does she smile? Her glass is empty and then full again and finally only half-empty when she awakes with Eugene standing over her. There is a terrible smell. She makes a motion to smooth her hair, but it is clotted with vomit. She retches again and tumbles from the sofa.

Eugene is picking her up in his strong arms. At first she struggles to get loose, but then she doesn't care any more, and as her head collapses against his shoulder, she tells herself that he is not Eugene. He is some stranger she has never met. A person, a man who cares for her, whom she can make happy, who will love her and let her have her child. He is not Eugene at all. He is . . . Virgil.

Carefully, as if he is bearing some fragile gift, Eugene carries her up the stairs to sleep and sleep and sleep.

5

It is 1970, July, and Adam Brockway is driving Mrs. Fayer to the bus station. She is leaving Hillside for good.

Adam is impossibly thin, with or without his clothes and Mrs. Fayer does not want to think of that. She wants to think of her new life on Marlborough Street, what it will be like; she wants to think of hope.

A beagle is crossing the road in front of the car and Mrs. Fayer's hand shoots out to keep herself from being thrown against the dashboard. But there is no need for her to worry since Adam has not even used the brakes. Has he accelerated the motor? The dog disappears, yelping, into the shrubbery. When Mrs. Fayer turns to glare at Adam, she discovers he is smiling.

"You almost killed that dog," she says. "Are you aware of that?"

"He moved in time," Adam says.

"But you didn't know if he would or not. You might have killed him."

"So? That's the breaks."

"The breaks." The men she has known. The fuckers. She sees the two bodies, naked, at the head of the stairs. "Tell me, Adam," she says, "what do you ever intend to do with your life? That is, if you don't kill yourself with your driving."

He turns a blank stare toward her. "I'm dying," he says in Mrs. Price's toneless voice. His face twists a little and then droops; he becomes Mrs. Price in the flesh as he repeats, "I'm dying."

"That's cruel," she says. "That's not funny."

"Yes, it is," he says, his voice angry. "It's funny."

He presses hard on the gas pedal and they drive in silence, going too fast on the country roads.

In this silence, Mrs. Fayer is back with Mrs. Price, leaving her again, this second time. Does she feel any guilt for what she is doing? No, she has an obligation to herself. And yet, poor Mrs. Price.

Jessie Price is over fifty now. Until her nervous breakdown and the stroke that followed it, she was a brilliant scholar, the author of several disturbing books, and a professor of philosophy at Vassar. It was the stroke that caused Jessie's friend to write to Mrs. Fayer. "Could you take her? She always said how much she loved you. She always said she owed you everything." Of course Mrs. Fayer could take her. And with that done, the friend was free to move on to another lover. Everybody Mrs. Price has loved ends up by leaving her. All human loves end.

"It doesn't matter what I do with my life," Adam says suddenly, breaking the silence, making Mrs. Fayer leave Mrs. Price yet again. "I'm going to be rich anyhow. My old man can disinherit me all he wants, but he can't do a thing about keeping me poor, because old Gramps left me a trust fund I'll be getting in two more years or so, and then, baby, it's Cadillac time."

"And so you can go through life," Mrs. Fayer says, angry herself now, "without doing anything, without giving anything, and everything just comes to you."

"That's right."

"Without asking and without thanks."

"That's how it is." Mrs. Fayer looks at him and Adam looks

back at her. She recognizes in those burnt eyes the rich glint of madness and for a moment she is terrified of him. "That's how it is," he says again. "Maybe you don't like it, but you've got no choice about accepting it."

Adam's voice is calm and hard, and his foot presses on the accelerator. The car leaps forward and then there is an intersection, a police car, a siren. Pounding the steering wheel with his fist, Adam grinds to a stop. After the lecture on speeding, the ticket, he turns to Mrs. Fayer and says, "You see? That's one thing that can't happen to you when you've got money. You can buy anything, even the police."

Mrs. Fayer sees the naked bodies, black and white, arms twining, hands moving on the taut flesh. She shakes her head.

"No, I don't accept it," she says.

6

It is a warm spring day in the year 1933. Jessica is three years married and nearly three months pregnant and, when she does not think of Eugene, she is almost happy. Something good will come from her disastrous marriage after all: a baby. She hums Gounod's "Ave Maria" as she washes the breakfast dishes.

Virgil Clark appears from the side of the house, on his way to the old cowbarn. There are no cows in the barn, there haven't been for years, so they use it as a place to park the car and store the chicken feed and put anything they don't know what to do with. The farm machinery is kept there; perhaps Virgil is going to plow the lower pasture.

Jessica smiles as she watches him stoop to pick something up. It must be a buttercup; they are early this year. She reaches with her soapy hands across the sink to the locked window. She can call to him from here. She can wave to him at least.

Before she has the window open, Virgil turns toward her and holds up the flower, as if he is lifting a toast to her. She waves. At once his large mouth opens and his white teeth flash as he returns her smile.

Her breath catches in her throat. Suddenly she sees their arms and legs tangled together and he is kissing her as his hand moves on her breast, on her throat. Everything goes dark for a moment.

And then Virgil is tapping with one finger at the window. She opens it further and he hands the flower through to her.

"A buttercup," he says, "this early."

"A beauty," she says.

They stand looking at each other through the raised window. His black hand rests on the white ledge.

"It's warm out here in the sun. You ought to come out."

"Yes."

"You ought to take a walk in the sun."

Jessica is thirty-three and pregnant as she stands at the window twirling the buttercup between her fingers. She is almost happy. Virgil has not yet turned to go.

"Are you going to plow the lower pasture?"

"Maybe. I'm going to check it. It might be too early yet."

"Yes."

"I'll check it. You should take a walk down there. It's always sunny down there."

"Yes."

They look at each other, saying nothing, until finally Jessica raises the flower and says, "Thank you." He nods and turns away, headed once again for the barn.

Virgil Clark. He is her friend, she trusts him. Virgil has worked at Hillside for just over a year, but he is the one person here Jessica feels close to. He showed up at the back door on the coldest day of winter and asked if he could chop firewood in exchange for a meal. "Yes," she said, and gave him the meal before she showed him the firewood that needed splitting. "Who's the nigger?" Eugene said when he saw him seated at the table, but afterward he was impressed by the way Virgil worked.

"Ever work a farm?" he asked.

"Uh huh," Virgil said.

"What kind of farm machinery do you know how to work?"

"What kind you got?"

"Damned uppity nigger," Eugene told Jessica, but he let

Virgil stay on anyway. Neither of them asked Virgil anything about himself, where he was from or if he had any family. He was just here, at Hillside, working on the farm and helping around the house when he was needed. Periodically there were spurts of anger, when Virgil refused to do what he had been told, or did it his own way. "He's got to go!" Eugene would shout, and then Jessica would have to make peace. She went to Virgil and scolded and wheedled and got him to agree to stay on. She went to Eugene and reasoned with him: they paid Virgil so little anyway, they couldn't manage to run the place without him, where else could they get such good help, and nearly free? "You and your damned nigger," Eugene would say, and then life at Hillside would go on as it had before.

Jessica watches him now as he turns from the window and heads toward the barn. She twists the yellow flower between her fingers, and she is thinking how his black skin gleams in the sun.

Virgil disappears into the barn and Jessica begins to sing a song she has heard on the radio. She is happy. She is almost happy. Perhaps this afternoon she will stroll down to the lower pasture and see if it is ready for plowing.

She has put out the lunch for Eugene and Virgil. She has collected the trays from the four old ladies. She has even gotten them settled in the afternoon sun. Virgil rises from the kitchen table and goes out. Eugene continues to sit there, drinking milk. He must be staring at her, waiting to start, but she keeps on scraping plates, her back to him. She has not bothered to eat lunch. She is not hungry, but for once she is not nauseous either. She hears the chair scrape; now he will start.

He leans on the counter, in her way, and he sniffs.

"No gin?" It is the first thing he has said to her all day.

"You're in my way."

"Ha!" and he goes, limping.

Well, he has done what he wanted to do. She is sick

now, frightened. But then she looks up and sees the buttercup, glassy yellow on the windowsill.

Eugene is the sick one, she tell herself, he is more unhappy than she. He is miserable, and he is transforming her into his own image and likeness.

She picks up the buttercup, still fresh, not even a little withered yet, and she holds it to her lips. She twirls it between her fingers.

Well, she will not be transformed into that. She will not be miserable like him; like him, a crusher of souls. That is one choice she will reject. "Yes," she says, "yes," and she washes the dishes more quickly now, because when she finishes she will stroll down past the barn to the lower pasture.

So she is past the barn now, past the chicken run, shading her eyes to see if she can locate Virgil. She sees him. At this distance he looks like a boy. The sun is hot on her shoulders and she slips off the old cardigan she has thrown around her. She feels young, she feels like running, but instead she steps off the path and walks slowly across the hard loam of the pasture. At once she can tell, by the way the ground feels beneath her feet, that it is too early for plowing. They could easily have another frost yet.

In the lower pasture the ground is softer. Virgil has seen her at a distance and has stopped thrusting at the rototiller. He leans on one of the round wooden arms and waits for her.

"It's too early," she calls from a little distance.

Virgil does not answer.

"Oh golly," she says, close to him now, "that's so rough, walking across the pasture. It's too early, isn't it."

"Watch," he says.

He bears down hard on the long arms of the rototiller and the topsoil rises in dark brown waves. He kicks the dirt aside and says, "See." Six inches down the earth is silvered with veins of frost. "You can get it all right, but it's a lot of work."

"It's too early," she says, patting his arm up near the shoulder. The muscle flexes beneath her touch. He must have enormous strength in that arm.

"There are some crocuses in the beech grove," he says, pointing beyond the little stream that marks the end of the pasture. "I saw them this morning."

"Oh, let's look," she says. "Is the stream too high?"

The melting snow has made the stream run fast and the stream bed has broadened to several feet.

"I'll never get across that," she says.

Virgil takes a short run and a long leap and he is on the other side.

"Come on," he says, "you can make it," but she knows she can't and so they walk downstream, one on each side of the water.

"There," he says. "There's a rock in the middle. You can jump to that and then across." Jessica looks at the rock doubtfully.

"Wait," he says. "I'll try it, to make sure it doesn't wobble. Here we go." He takes a long step to the center of the stream, his weight suspended over the water, and then he shoves off from the bank, and lands with both feet on the rock. For a second he loses his balance; his arms windmill and he seems about to fall backward, but then he rights himself. He jiggles the rock like a seesaw, throwing his weight from front to back. "Well, it's not bad," he says. And he takes another long step toward the bank where Jessica stands, laughing. The rock twists to the side and as he tries to push off from it, the rock slides from under him. His arms flail wildly and he spills backward and lands full length in the icy rushing water.

Jessica covers her face with her hands. Has he struck his head on a stone? Will the water suddenly run red as he lies there unconscious?

Virgil is sitting in the stream, laughing and laughing. She

laughs with him. It is all wonderfully funny now: the teetering rock, Virgil trying to catch his balance, the dunking in the stream. She laughs and claps her hands.

"Are you all right?" she says, worried but laughing still. "Are you hurt?"

"Oh, shit!" he says, standing up in the rushing water. "Shee-it." His clothes stick to him, glistening wet.

On the bank Virgil shakes himself like a dog. He barks, performing for her.

"I shouldn't laugh," she says. "But it's so funny. Why is it so funny?"

"Because it happened to somebody else," and they both laugh because they know he is right.

"You'll catch your death," she says.

And then they take the long way back to the house, following the path the full length of the meadow as it winds up the hill to the barn. They walk slowly, shoulder to shoulder. Virgil drags the rototiller, prongs up, with his left hand; he gestures now and then with his right. The sun is hot on their backs. It is one of those early spring days that are really a false summer. It will not last.

From where he stands on the back porch, Eugene can see the two figures approach even at a great distance. Jessica is swinging something in her hand; her old cardigan. Virgil is dragging the rototiller and gesturing off to the right. They are walking slowly, talking. She laughs, tossing her head, as he says things to her. And she is pregnant.

As they round the barn they notice him. He is wearing his suit. Jessica's smile disappears and at the same moment Virgil turns from her and goes to the barn.

Eugene shoots looks back and forth between them. He has too many things he wants to say—about gin, about niggers, about rolling in the hay—but they are all crowded out by her laughter. She is happy.

They go into the house without a word.

Jessica knows that if he is dressed like this, it means he is going to Springfield. She no longer cares—or so she tells herself. Springfield is only thirty miles distant, but for Eugene it is another world. He has friends there, men like himself who have been in the war, who drink and grow friendlier, who grow intimate and drink some more, and then they go out together and find women. They fuck them and then fall asleep. The women do not mind, though one or two sometimes object that they are not allowed, not even asked, to demonstrate more unusual talents; but what does it matter; it's a living. In the morning the men go off and drink and grow friendlier, and the cycle continues. These binges have lasted as long as a week, never less than two or three days, they last as long as the money from his disability check holds out. "Find them, fuck them, forget them," Eugene told his wife when he returned from the first Springfield trip following their marriage. "No!" she said, crying, "I don't want to hear!" and she ran from the room. Eugene shrugged, understanding. They had been married less than a month.

And now he is wearing his suit, which means he must be going to Springfield.

"Well?" she says.

"*You're* awfully happy," he says. He wants to go on, to strike at her somehow, but he cannot get beyond the word happy. Is he angry that she has something from which he is shut out? Is he jealous? Does he remember what she has given him and realize it is gone now? Perhaps he has a glimpse of something that will happen: himself dying and Jessica standing at the foot of the bed, a small laugh building in her throat? There is no way of knowing.

"Yes," she says, "I *am* happy."

"Jessica." His voice is warm, pleading. "Jessica, think for a minute. Come on now, let's sit down and talk for a minute. We have to talk." He guides her to the kitchen table, and they sit down facing one another. He coughs. "Now let's be reasonable about this. Let me just finish what I have to say before you say anything, all right? All right. The thing is this. This is 1933! We have no money, we have nothing, and everything's getting worse every day. You and I, the only way we can possibly keep this place together is if we both work, and Virgil. Without you, what would I do? Be reasonable, Jessica."

"Yes?"

"Well, that's why I'm asking you, don't have the baby."

"I'm having it."

"There you go, you never let me finish. You never listen to the opposite side." His voice goes thin with anger. "We can't manage, Jessica. Can't you get that through your head? We can barely feed the four old bags as it is, let alone ourselves. And if you're sick, or if you've got to spend all your time with a baby, we just can't do it."

"Why? What is it about you, Eugene? There's something you're not saying. I think back to any conversation we've ever had about children and always there's the same unreasoning hatred of them. No, not hatred. It's something else, something, oh, I don't know. Yes, I do know. It's fear. You're afraid."

She looks at him and his face changes; she knows she has hit on it. Or at least she has come near.

"But why?" she asks. "What is there to fear about a baby, about having a baby? I don't understand."

"You're crazy."

"No, I'm not. And you know I've hit on it." She is ahead now; she is on top.

"You haven't hit on anything."

"What are you afraid of?" She is not asking him, she is asking herself. But he is getting up; he is not going to be caught by her. Her tricks. "Or is it sex?" she says, not having thought it until she has said it. Hearing herself, she turns the words over in her mind. But if he is afraid of sex, how is it that he is so fierce and rough with her? Or why does he go to Springfield and do whatever he does with those women?

Perhaps she is wrong. Perhaps she knows nothing about what makes people fear or hate or love. "Are you afraid I'd have something to love that isn't you? Something of my own?"

She looks up at him, but he is gone. She turns, confused, from the sink to the table and back again. Suddenly he is in the room with her, in one of his rages, and he is speaking softly.

"Where I am going," he says, "is Springfield. And before I come back I will locate a nice friendly doctor who will take care of you and that is the end of that."

"Do it," she says. "Do it. But I won't go to him, and if he comes here, he'll discover only you and the four women, because I'll be gone."

Eugene pauses, a deathly pause, waiting for her to look at him.

"There are other ways, Jessica." He is white. "Did you ever stop to think of what happens after the baby is born? Did you ever stop to think of how many accidents can happen to a baby, a little tiny baby? Babies have been known to smother in their own little pillows. There they are sleeping away, peaceful as anything, and the next morning, phhht! Anything could happen to your little baby. Accidents happen every day, Jessica."

Her face betrays nothing.

"Don't wait up for me," he says. "I may be late."

• • •

Jessica drinks gin.

She is in the present, in 1933, and she has cause to drink.

First she lets something happen in her mind, click, and then she is able to drift, vague and distracted already, toward the medicine closet and the bottle of gin. She does not think what it is that happens in her mind; it is important not to.

Then the hand closes on the bottle, the hand reaches for the glass, the sharp odor of gin, the sting in her mouth and nostrils, and, after a few minutes, dullness.

Dullness is what Jessica wants, or so she thinks, and she does what she can to get it. All feeling suspended, the mind numbed against intrusions, against itself. Nothing.

"Nothing," she says, reading the note on the bottle. For medicinal use only. "Nothing."

Sister Judith bends over her prayer book while the singing rises around her. She is twenty-one, admitted at last to her vows of poverty, chastity, holy obedience. Her own rich contralto voice is silent. She is praying. In a moment she will vow herself to God, forever.

Mrs. Fayer is sprawled on the cobblestones in Louisburg Square, looking at her torn photographs and holy cards lying in the gutter.

Everything is in a process of transformation: nothing stays itself.

Finally she is drunk. The mind has dulled some time ago, and now the senses fail to register. She can hear almost nothing, and even what she does hear has no meaning. A clock ticking. One of the old women snoring. A car going past on the road. These are empty sounds. What could they mean? She smells nothing. The house could burn down and she would not know it. Touch, taste, sight: all of them go. And she is safe, at last.

She is dead.

• • •

Jessica is going upstairs to Virgil's room above the garage. It has got to happen.

Eugene has said, "Don't wait up for me; I may be late," and he has driven off to Springfield to find a doctor. A friendly one. For a long while after he left, his words rattled in her mind. She must not listen. She must not give in. And so she made sauce for the spaghetti, she dustmopped the entire first floor, she scrubbed the three bathrooms. But the words came back and back. "Accidents happen every day, Jessica." She lay in the bathtub in scalding water. "Think of how many accidents can happen to a baby, a little tiny baby."

And then she let whatever it is, click, happen in her mind, and she went to the medicine closet, and now she is nearly drunk.

Jessica is going upstairs to Virgil's room above the garage.

She tells herself she is cooking dinner the way she always has. But she has splashed spaghetti sauce all over the stove. There are red spots on the counter, on the kitchen floor, and she has cooked the spaghetti almost to mush. She serves the old women in their rooms. She serves Virgil at the kitchen table. She does not eat, again she is not hungry.

"I'm fine," she says, as he tries to help her with the dishes. "Let that alone. I'm perfectly fine." She frowns at him as he turns off the gas jet she has left burning. "Get out," she says, in a voice she has never used to him. Nigger, she thinks, but she watches from the window as he takes the path near the barn.

Death would end all this.

"Nigger," she says, and her tears fall into the dishwater as, slowly, painfully, she cleans the plates and puts them in the rack.

The effects of the gin are wearing off. Jessica is more desperate now. Virgil has come into the house an hour ago, two hours ago, and has gone up the back stairs to his room above the garage. Not a word to her. Nor has she apologized for what she said, for what she thought.

"Eugene," she says, pacing up and down the corridor. "Eugene," to the darkened parlor windows. Across the road, the steep hill and the meadow have disappeared in a thick mist. She cannot see even to the end of the front lawn. Last winter, when she was not expecting a child, she saw three deer in that meadow, a buck and two young does. The gin has worn off completely. She should apologize to Virgil. She wants desperately to talk to Virgil, to somebody. What if she were to run screaming from the house, her red hair flying in the cold night air? What if she were just to disappear in the mist like that meadow? Or she could walk to the lower pasture and lie, face down, in the water. She feels it for a moment rushing about her, rushing into her. She is freezing cold. What if . . . but then, miraculously, the mist clears and she can see beyond the front lawn, beyond the road. There, in a thin white shaft of moonlight, halfway up the steep hill, stands the buck she remembers. His head is lifted, tense, as if he knows he is being watched. The enormous spreading antlers flash black and silver in the moonlight. Near him stand the two does, grazing.

Jessica catches her breath. She is not drunk; she is not imagining things; the three deer are there. And then, in a second, they are gone. The mist closes over them. The hill recedes, and then the road, and finally there is only the dark window giving back the reflection of her parted lips and her warm and shining eyes.

"I'll tell Virgil," she says, as if she has at last found the solution to her problems. "Yes," she says. And she goes up the stairs to his room above the garage.

Jessica hurries. She tells herself that she must tell Virgil about the deer. She will tap at his door, it will open, and she will tell him. Once she has told him, everything will be different. She does not know how it will be different, but she is certain it will be. Everything. Her heart races and she throws back her hair, which hangs loose and makes her look young. "I'll tell him about the deer," she says, and she tries not to think, I am young and I am alive. "I'll tell him."

She does not tell him, because there is no time, there is no need. They are lying on the bed, gasping. Virgil's black hand curves around her breast, the thumb moving against the pink nipple. He has waited patiently for this and smiles now as he looks at the ceiling. When his breathing has come back to normal, though hers has not, he says, "The second time is better, isn't it."

"Both," she says.

He laughs and draws her closer.

Later she says, "I love you and I don't know anything

about you. I don't know where you're from. I don't know who you are. Tell me."

"It has to be love, doesn't it," he says. "You have to tell yourself it's love." He hears her make that little gasping sound and feels her whole body go rigid. "All right," he says "call it love. Lies help, sometimes."

"Tell me," she says.

And Virgil tells her. He tells her only part of the truth: that his grandfather was a slave and his father an evangelist; that he is twenty-eight years old; that his wife has died in childbirth and the child too is dead. He does not tell her the whole truth: that he is wanted by the police for raping a white woman in Chicago, Illinois; that he slept with that woman because she came to his room the way Jessica has come to his room; that he will leave Hillside before Jessica has an attack of conscience and decides she too has been raped. He tells her part of the truth and he makes up the rest. He is a good liar.

They have talked for an hour, or rather Virgil has talked and Jessica has listened, murmuring to him, saying small things into his chest and the hollow of his arm. Her hands explore his body, shyly at first. "Cock," he says, and makes her say it after him, and saying it, she becomes more adventurous, doing new things with her hands, with her mouth, with the curves and recesses of her own body. She has never before thought of such things and now she is doing them. She is enjoying them. She does not talk of love as she discovers a whole new world of flesh. She does not talk at all. "You love it, don't you!" he says. "You were born for it." She is panting, sweating. "Fuck me," she says. He is lying on his back and she sits upright straddling his thighs, facing him. "Fuck me," and she plunges down on him, riding and riding him into a changed present.

Before dawn he carries her back to her room. Both of them are naked and they laugh that he can carry her—their black and white flesh twining, mingling—naked through the house where four old women lie asleep. From his room above the garage, through the storeroom and the kitchen, through the corridor, up the stairs and into the bedroom she shares with Eugene Henderson Fayer; how many times do they make this endless journey? She knows.

She does not awaken until nearly noon. She serves the four old women a late breakfast, which will have to do them for lunch as well. She does her kitchen work, she washes, she cleans, but she cannot distract herself from the resolution forming at the back of her mind. Virgil must leave.

Slowly, thoughtfully, she goes up the stairs to Virgil's room. She will ask him to leave. He has to. She was out of her mind last night, she will say, she was crazy. She can give him money; she will borrow it, but he must go away. At the head of the stairs she rests, terrified at what she has begun. She feels the ache between her legs, she touches her bruised mouth: these things can never be undone.

But Virgil is gone. There is no sign, other than the rumpled sheets on the floor, that anyone has ever lived here, that Jessica and Virgil Clark have done the things they have done. He has simply disappeared.

Jessica is filled with exhilaration, with a wild joy. Now everything is possible. She will not have to tell Eugene; she will not be found out. She can have her baby like any ordinary woman, and she can forget the terrible love-making, the sex. "Fuck," she says and shakes her head against the memory. It was crazy. It was absurd. No, she is not like that. That woman is not who she is. She was a nun and now she is married and pregnant. She does not know who she is, but she knows she is not that woman.

Tiredness falls away from her; the worry, the terror are gone. She claps her hands once as she turns away forever, she thinks, from Virgil's room. Jessica is young and alive and she takes the stairs two at a time.

And then it happens.

On the last stair she trips; she is falling. She tries to regain balance and she is flung, but this is not possible, against the bannister. She suffers only a slight blow on the stomach, so slight that afterwards there is not even a bruise. But her leg is wet with something, blood?, and she is dizzy. She has to sit down. She has to lie down.

In less than an hour her miscarriage is over with.

She is a nurse who has worked in pediatrics, and she knows this sort of thing never happens, cannot happen. She herself has taken care of a woman eight months pregnant who was beaten by her husband. She has taken care of more than one woman who has fallen down a full flight of stairs. And always the babies have survived. It is not possible to trip on a single stair and lose a child.

It is not possible, but it is what has happened to her nonetheless.

7

"You'd better give her a shot," the voice says. "Fifteen mgs of morphine. Give it i.m."

"Right away," the other voice says.

So she must be in the hospital. Yes, the walls, the tile floors, that smell of disinfectant and of flesh decaying. She is Sister Judith and she is thirty years old. For her there is nothing but the present, because she is in love, she is loved.

She is walking down the corridor in her starched white habit. Her skirts rustle in a way she has never noticed before. Is it the blue apron she wears that makes the rustling sound? She tries to concentrate on the sound, to keep all other thoughts away.

Sister Judith has known Eugene Henderson Fayer for less than a month and she is going to leave the convent and marry him. She has decided this already, though she does not know it yet.

Eugene Henderson Fayer. Eugene Henderson Fayer. Her skirts rustle and she tries to concentrate on the sound. Eugene. She has just been relieved by another Sister and now she can go to chapel and pray. She is going to make the most important decision of her life, she thinks, not knowing she has already made it, and so she must pray for guidance.

"Dear Jesus," she begins, her eyes fixed on the huge crucifix suspended over the altar. She gazes with love at the white and twisted body of Christ on the cross, the arms almost out of the shoulder joints, but she sees only the handsome mouth and strong chin of Eugene Henderson Fayer, who needs her.

She is a nun, she has never known any other life. And now she is going to marry. Yes.

She kneels, praying for guidance to do the right thing.

8

Mrs. Fayer is about to purchase her ticket for the bus to Boston. Her heart beats faster as she approaches the ticket counter, even though she has done this twice before during the past month, first to arrange for the new apartment on Marlborough Street, and then again to test herself. Does she truly want to get away from Hillside? Does she want to live in Boston? She is not sure what she wants, but she knows that what she has is not it.

The day is that same day again, always in the present, a mild day in July of 1970 when she leaves the Hillside Rest Home. It is the day she sees Martha and Adam naked on the landing. It is the day she meets Lulu Mercer, finally, for the first time. It is the day she lies on the sidewalk, dying, no not dying, and says to the black policeman crouching above her, "Enter me." It is only one day in her present and she is not yet done with it. She must do the next thing, which is to purchase her ticket.

The girl behind the ticket counter snaps her chewing gum as she talks to a young man with a broom.

"Yeah, well, screw you," she says. "You know what you can do, you can go screw yourself."

The young man with the broom makes a gesture that is lost on Mrs. Fayer. The girl lets out a shriek of laughter. She looks at Mrs. Fayer who says, "One way to Boston, please," and then turns back to the young man. "Yeah, well, you know what you can do?" He moves away, laughing. "See ya, Larry," she calls after him. She snaps her gum methodically as she follows him with her eyes.

"One way to Boston, please."

The girl pulls a face and slaps the ticket on the counter. "Three-ninety." She is looking over Mrs. Fayer's shoulder, pouting. "Don't you have nothing smaller?" she says, waving the ten dollar bill Mrs. Fayer has handed her. "Christ!" And in a moment, "Here's your change," placing a dime and a pile of ones on top of the ticket. "Now I'll have to get more change," she says, accusing, and slams the drawer of the register. As Mrs. Fayer moves away from the ticket counter she can hear the girl shouting to someone named Artie for more fives and ones.

The girl is young, sixteen perhaps, and already she is bored to death. Is death everywhere?

Mrs. Fayer's breath is short and that sharp pain is back again. She wants to sit down, to lie down.

"What are you doing?" Adam Brockway is standing beside her holding her suitcase. He has parked the car and is waiting now to see her off on the bus.

"What are you doing?" he asks again.

Mrs. Fayer has been turning back and forth like a lost child.

"I'm running in circles," she says. "What do you think I'm doing."

"There's two seats over there," he says, "by the glass doors."

Mrs. Fayer follows him as he moves easily through the people and baggage. He could be any one of a number of young men in the bus station. They are all dressed the same way, in jeans and workshirts, and their hair is long and not very clean. But he is Adam Brockway, he is not the others. Perhaps he is not even like the others. He has taken drugs of all kinds, she knows that, but he does not take drugs any longer. And what does she care if he and Martha do those things in the room above the garage. It is none of her affair. After today, she will never see either of them again.

Mrs. Fayer eases into the gray plastic chair and for a moment her vision blurs. Everyone seems to be looking at her, every face turned in her direction, assessing, criticizing. They know her and she doesn't know them, not any of them. She blinks at the sharp pain behind her eyes and then everything clears and she sees an ordinary bus station with people reading magazines, fussing with children, staring. But not at her. Just staring the way people do in bus stations, with idle curiosity, with the intention of not being caught.

"Get a look at that one," Adam says, following her gaze. "She'd fit right in at Hillside."

What is Adam doing here? Why doesn't he leave?

Mrs. Fayer realizes that she herself has been staring at a woman at the end of the row of chairs facing them. She is a heavy woman, and old, seventy at least. Her age is exaggerated by the countless little curls that dangle in perfect order across her forehead. It is the hairstyle Shirley Temple wore when she sang about the good ship *Lollipop,* and it makes the old woman look preposterous. Her hands chop the air and the curls bob on her forehead as she talks rapidly to a black woman whose hands are folded in her lap and whose gaze is fixed somewhere beyond the glass doors. The woman reminds her of someone. Who? Is it a Sister? Is it Sister Veronica?

Mrs. Fayer watches as the woman's hands move in the air, carving complaints and injustices; she has heard that kind over and over. No, she is not Sister Veronica. And yes, she would fit right in at Hillside.

"Hey, are you all right?" Adam says.

"She's not funny any more than Mrs. Price is funny."

"But you're interested in her, aren't you. Why are you interested?"

Adam is not stupid. He has gone to private schools, to Choate. He is a Brockway and he will inherit the Brockway money. Her name is Fayer and she has inherited . . . what? She is too old for this, and what does it matter anyway? The meek will not inherit the earth; the scavengers will, the rat-faced takers who do nothing but destroy. She has seen it all.

"Why are you interested?" Adam points at the old woman with the curls on her forehead.

"*Humanus sum, nil alienum mihi,*" she says. So she is involved after all.

"Latin! Far out! How'd you ever learn Latin?"

"I went to school, Adam. We had schools even in the dark ages when I was a girl."

"Fantastic! What does it mean, what you said?"

"It means, 'as the twig is bent, so grows the tree.' That's a free translation, but accurate."

Adam looks at her with appreciation, he is amused, and she fumbles in her purse for a tissue. So she has come to this, quoting Eugene to impress—no, to insult—a spoiled child. But this was not why she said it; she does not know why she said it.

"You're all right," Adam says. "Funny that we never talked."

Over the loudspeaker a muffled voice announces the bus for Boston ready for boarding.

"Everything is funny, isn't it." She has decided to make the parting ugly. She stands and reaches for her bag, but he gets to it first. He walks her to the boarding platform.

"Don't be sore," he says. "I tell you what, I'll look you up in Boston. We'll get together."

"Do, yes. When you've finished your book."

How could she know about his book, that book he would write once he got his money? There is no way she could know, and yet she has just said it. He pretends she didn't say it; she couldn't have said it.

"Another zinger, right? Take it slow, Mrs. Fayer. You're okay."

She takes a seat by the window and leans back, closing her eyes until her anger passes. Almost at once there is a sharp knock at the window. Adam is there, grinning and blowing kisses. He is making a fool of her. She does not look at him. She stares at her hands, folded in her lap. But the knocking at the window gets louder and louder. People on the bus turn to look. Adam is beating at the window now with his fists. He is shouting at her. The driver drops the bags he is shoving into the luggage compartment and tells Adam to stop, but Adam only beats louder at the window. "Goddamn you, look at me," he is shouting, but Mrs. Fayer stares down at her folded hands. He must be mad. He must be dangerous. A gang of bus drivers, four of them and then five, drag Adam away from the bus. One of them is punching him hard in the back. People outside are watching to see what they will do to him. People inside can see only a little, so they turn and stare at Mrs. Fayer. Her eyes are closed now. She is waiting for it to end. Everything ends.

Finally the bus begins to back out of its berth. But then it stops and the driver jerks open the door to let one late passenger get on. It is the woman with the little curls.

Mrs. Fayer closes her eyes, but that does no good. Lulu Mercer has found her.

"My name is Lulu Mercer."

"Yes."

"Lulu Mercer." She beams and speaks louder.

Mrs. Fayer watches as Lulu Mercer crams a shopping bag into the luggage rack above the seat and then struggles out of her coat. She folds the coat neatly, precisely, and puts it too up on the rack. And then, having settled a large leather carry-all at her feet, she plumps heavily into the seat with Mrs. Fayer.

"Well, now," she says, eager for conversation. "*Ms.* Lulu Mercer, that is. My Henry is gone to the everlasting, God rest his soul, I always say. He's five months dead, Henry. So I've become a Ms. Like this, m-z-z."

Mrs. Fayer shifts a little in her seat and tries to look out the window. She is dizzy again. There are tiny beads of sweat on her forehead. Perhaps it is the swaying of the bus. No, it is Lulu Mercer.

"And your name? I didn't catch your name. I always say that a bus trip is for making friends." She pauses, reflecting. "A bus trip is for making friends. Now that's something you'll remember. You'll hear that, oh, maybe not in five years, maybe not in ten years, maybe twenty, but some day you'll hear that, and you'll stop and cock your head to one side like a bright little bird and say, I've heard that somewhere before. Sure enough, you'll say. Lulu Mercer said that!"

Mrs. Fayer studies the pantomime of herself remembering Lulu Mercer some twenty years from now—at ninety—and she marvels at the foolishness of the woman. She stretches her legs out straight; let someone else worry about crazy people like Lulu Mercer. She has no responsibility for the Adam Brockways or the Lulu Mercers of this world. She is free of all of them. Like a bright little bird, indeed, and in spite of herself, she smiles.

Lulu Mercer pounces on the smile. "There now. You see? You'll see. You're just like me. Now, what's your name, dear?"

"Mrs. Fayer."

"I mean your full name."

"Mrs. Eugene Henderson Fayer."

"Eugene Henderson! Well, I can't very well call you that, can I? What'll I call you?"

"You can call me Mrs. Fayer for short."

"Oh, but *Mrs.* is out. Nobody is a Mrs. any more, not if you're a widow, and it looks to me like you're a widow. You a widow?"

Mrs. Fayer says nothing.

"Sure, just like I thought. So you should be a *Ms.* M-z-z. You should be Ms. Henderson or Ms. Connolly or whatever you were before you married Eugene. Now take me. I was Lulu Mercer before I became . . ."

"Connolly? Did you say Connolly?"

"Henderson or Connolly, I said. You've got that Irish look."

"Oh."

"Don't you worry, we've all got something. The Lord never gives us a heavier cross than we can bear, I always say." Lulu Mercer recoils a little and adjusts her glasses, bringing Mrs. Fayer into sharp focus. "Ms. Fair. Well, now that's a real pretty name. Fair is an excellent name because it means you're just, you know, honest, well . . . fair. And at the same time it means pretty. Now that's what I call an excellent name."

"We spell it F–a–y–e–r."

"Oh, well, that's different. Don't mind anyway. It's going to be a nice trip just the same. You from Springfield, Ms. Fayer?"

"No."

"Don't be formal, just call me Lulu. Everybody calls me Lulu. Lulu Mercer, that's me. Then you must be from Boston. Boston?"

"Mmmm."

"Where would that be now in Boston? I know Boston like the back of my hand, grew up in Boston, or on the outskirts really, West Roxbury. That's where I met my Henry, God rest his soul, when he was still in med school. Highland Avenue, West Roxbury. I made him everything he was. Everything. He knew it too. He'd always say, 'Who made me everything I am today? Lulu Mercer, that's who.' So where would that be in Boston?" She turns to face Mrs. Fayer who has closed her eyes. "You're not asleep are you, Ms. Fayer?" She nudges her. "Are you asleep?"

Without opening her eyes, Mrs. Fayer says, "I'm very tired. I thought I'd rest a bit."

"Of course, dear, you rest. You have a nice little rest for yourself. I'll just talk."

Lulu Mercer is talking and talking and Mrs. Fayer has no choice but to be there. But she is not there now; she is on the cobblestone pavement of Louisburg Square. Her head aches and her hand is bleeding where she has scraped it. She reaches for the nearest photograph. It shows the headpiece and the warm eyes of Sister Veronica, dead for five years now. There is a white lacy effect where the picture has been torn across the nose. She picks up another. It is of the handsome mouth and jutting chin of her husband Eugene. Another: Dr. Turner. And Gordon; only Gordon has escaped whole. She drops the photographs and leans her head once more against the iron post, grateful to be alive. Her heart swells with gratitude. Her heart fills her whole chest, her body.

She wakes struggling to breathe. With the ball of her fist she smooths the place beneath her breast where her heart must be. She feels nothing, only a knot there. Somewhere Lulu Mercer is talking, a loud voice keeping noise in the air. And then, it passes. She is not having a heart attack after all. Not yet.

"I'm on the bus to Boston," she whispers, grounding herself in the present.

"Of course you are, dear. We're both on the bus to Boston. Now, tell me about your kiddies."

"What? Kiddies?" The knot beneath her breast has been replaced by a hot pain. If only she could get a breath of fresh air. If only she could get back to the walled garden where she walked with Sister Veronica. She gasps, and looks hard at Lulu Mercer. "What are you talking about? What kiddies?"

"Well, landsakes, children is what I'm talking about! I saw you in the bus station with your son, he was seeing you off, and what I am asking is do you have any more than just the one son?"

"He's not my son. Adam is nothing to me."

"Now, you take me. I love kiddies, always have, always will. But it just wasn't my lot to have any of my own, not with Henry. Henry was busy elsewhere, if you take my meaning." Lulu Mercer lowers her voice, but it becomes more urgent, more intense. "He took up with another woman, a tramp. She was a nobody. He drank with her; they'd get drunk, and then they'd do filthy things together. She'd make him. That's how some women are. It's natural for them; it's normal. And my Henry was weak; he had the weakness of the flesh, God rest his soul. But I stuck with him to the end. That's how I am. That's me, Lulu Mercer faithful to the end."

She pulls back, tapping her chest with her fist as if admitting some awful weakness, and then she leans forward again. Her eyes narrow behind her glasses and her face hardens as she leans over Mrs. Fayer.

"But her, that tramp, she'll never get away from me. I'll hound her to her grave. She thought she could win, but she was wrong. I won. She wanted the money. She wanted to be the doctor's wife, but that's who I was and that's who I stayed right up to the end. But now I'm me, me, Ms. Lulu Mercer. And don't worry, I've got it all written down." She thumps the leather carry-all at her feet. "Every rotten word she ever said to me."

Mrs. Fayer stares at the transformation. Lulu Mercer's face is yellow and cracked under a heavy layer of powder and her tiny eyes are made smaller by her thick glasses. But in her fury the furrows and the marks of age seem to fall away and her face becomes a death mask. It could be made of iron. This is not a human face at all.

"He brought that tramp into my home to fight with me. But I fixed her, I've got it all written down. I've got the proof right here in my bag." She wrenches the bag into her lap and unzips it. "Here and here and here," she says, pulling out envelopes stuffed with scraps of paper, all of them covered in tiny handwriting. "I've got it all written down. Look! Just look at this! It's my life. My whole life is in these notes. I never let them out of my sight. I read them over nights and I add to them whenever I remember more. I've got it locked here in my heart, God knows, but I've got it on paper too." Lulu Mercer plunges her hand into the carry-all and brings out a handkerchief with which she dabs at her forehead and upper lip. It is a small square of white linen with three little strawberries embroidered in one corner. "There could be a trial," she says, "I'd go to trial tomorrow if they'd let me. I'd be glad to be judged, because . . . do you know why? Because I know that any court in the United States of America, so help me God, would say, Lulu Mercer, you're to blame!" She pauses for dramatic effect. "You're to blame for being too good to them. You were too good. That's your one failing."

"Don't. I . . ."

"She's the one to blame, that no-good, she's to blame for the whole thing. We'd never have been separated if it wasn't for her. It would always be just me and Henry, in love. He loved me. His love belonged to me, and she stole it. I told Henry, I said to him, the electric chair is too good for her. Too good." She leans across Mrs. Fayer until their faces almost touch. "I said, and I mean it, they should pull out that tongue of hers and slice it off piece by piece. I could do it, if they were afraid. God would give me the strength." She leans back, breathing heavily. "But they didn't get the money. Not from Lulu Mercer, they didn't."

Mrs. Fayer cannot take her eyes from this woman. She is insane surely. "Please," she says, "please just don't talk for a while. I'm not feeling myself."

"Oh, of course, you poor dear. I know. I know. You're just like me. You go ahead and close your eyes. You're in the hands of Ms. Lulu Mercer. You're going to be all right, you're going to be just fine." She stops talking at last and lays her head back against the cushions where she can watch Mrs. Fayer breathing in and out. A smile creeps across her mouth. "I'll see you get to Boston nice and safe."

Mrs. Fayer falls into a deep dreamless sleep. She is a child in that walled garden she cannot return to and she is walking with Sister Veronica. She is Jessica Connolly.

"Ours is a life lived for others, Jessica. A Sister's life is not her own. It is God's, first of all, and then it belongs to anyone who needs it. To be a nun is the highest calling a woman can have, and it is the most painful. We are alone with God and his love is fire."

Jessica is eleven years old and in love. She listens to Sister Veronica say "his love is fire" and she repeats it to herself over and over. Sister Veronica's habit makes a swishing sound as she walks up and down the cloister path; the long string of rosary beads that hang from her waist clicks whenever the beads touch. Jessica listens to these sounds as she repeats to herself "his love is fire." The sun is warm on her shoulders as she walks beside the nun, up and down the paths of the walled garden. But when she turns her face up to Sister Veronica's, she discovers not the face she knows and loves, but the iron mask of Lulu Mercer.

Someone is bending over her, pinching her arm. "Ms. Fayer. Ms. Fayer?" the voice says. "I have to get off here. Chestnut Hill. But I'll be seeing you in Boston, because we're not nearly done with yet."

Mrs. Fayer is wide awake now and stares the woman down. "Louise Turner is in a mental home in Lenox," she says.

Lulu Mercer's smile narrows. "I'm not that woman. That woman—that Louise Turner—is a crazy woman. They had to lock her up. I'm Lulu Mercer. *Ms.* Lulu Mercer, that's who."

"You are *not* Louise Turner."

"I'll be seeing you, Ms. Fayer. I'll find you."

She is gone, but then in a second she is back again.

"There are no coincidences, Ms. Fayer. There are no coincidences at all."

When the bus reaches the terminal in Park Square, Mrs. Fayer wakes to find herself alone. Her head throbs and again there is a hard knot below her left breast.

9

It is New Year's Day, 1935. Jessica will remember it; she will never leave it.

She is standing beside Dr. Turner as they listen to Eugene's labored breathing. He has pneumonia and is only semi-conscious much of the time. With his damaged lungs, there is every likelihood the pneumonia will kill him; Jessica knows this.

Dr. Turner motions her out of the room. He is only four years older than she, but he is fatherly with all his patients and especially with Jessica. He has known Eugene for years and he has some idea what Jessica's marriage must be like. And he is fond of her; it pains him to see what she is doing to herself. Outside the room, he puts both hands on her shoulders so that she can feel the weight of what he is saying.

"He's in a bad way, Jess. Those powders—the sulfa—he's got to have one every four hours." Dr. Turner pauses for emphasis. "It could mean his life."

"His life," she says, nodding.

The powders are vile, they poison the taste of everything. She put the first one in his milk, but he refused to drink it. After that she mixed the powder in applesauce, which smothers the taste. He has been on the powders for three days now.

"If he makes it through the night, chances are he'll make it altogether. Remember, every four hours."

"Every four hours," Jessica says.

"What I mean is," and here his voice drops to a whisper, "go easy on the gin, Jessie." Dr. Turner kisses her on the forehead and starts down the stairs. "I'll come by in the morning," he says over his shoulder.

She watches him out of sight and then goes to the bedroom window where she can see him getting into his car. Although his shoulders are stooped inside his dark blue suit, he looks very young from this distance. He has a large shock of blond hair and a bushy mustache, but not too bushy. It is just right for his face. He swings his black bag across the front seat and then gets in and backs the car slowly out of the driveway. He is a good man and he is right about the gin. She must not. Eugene's life depends on it.

Later, as she is feeding him his applesauce, Eugene says to her, "It could mean my life." Her eyes grow large for a second, but there is no emotion in them. "Yes, I heard him. It could mean my life." Eugene lies back on the pillows studying her. When he breathes, there is a rattle in his lungs; his eyes are bright with fever. "This could be your chance to get rid of me." Suddenly he writhes in the bed, choking, and spits up a huge chunk of phlegm. He lies back, exhausted, breathing heavily. "Did you hear me, Jessica?"

"May God forgive you."

Eugene sleeps for a little while, or perhaps it is a long while. Jessica thinks of what he has said; that she could let him die, that she could murder him. He is cruel, mindless. She tells herself it is the fever, that he doesn't know what he is saying. But she knows. She knows.

She waits for the rage to mount, for that click in her head, and then she drifts down the stairs and into the kitchen and watches while her hand reaches for the bottle of cleansing gin. And then she drifts back up the stairs to keep watch.

"And so you've got your way at last," Eugene says, his voice barely a whisper. His face is white. His eyes have sunk in his head so that they look hooded and his full mouth has become a thin slit.

"It's what you've always wanted."

"What?"

"To see me like this, helpless, useless."

"No."

"To have me at your mercy."

"No," she says. She is unwilling to speak because of the gin; she knows she will slur her words.

She turns from him and stares at the carpet. It is an imitation Persian with arabesques of orange and green and burgundy. She squints, trying not to think of him, and the colors on the floor move. She is transforming them into different shapes merely by shutting her eyes a little. The green and the orange fuse; what color is it? Everything is fluid, changing, as the arabesques run together and overlap. And she is doing it, transforming color into color, making the curved lines straight. Nothing holds. Nothing is the same from second to second.

She hears the voice in the room. Is it his voice or her own? Nothing will ever be the same after tonight.

"Isn't it?" he insists.

"Isn't what?"

"Isn't it what you've always wanted?"

"I never wanted that. I don't want it now."

She lets the arabesques in the carpet fall back into their old forms and she looks him straight in the eye. He turns to the wall and smiles bitterly.

"Never," she says.

"The baby," he says. "You've never forgiven me for it."

He does not mention Virgil because he has never believed what she told him. But he has mentioned the baby and that is enough.

There is a blinding flash across her eyes, light from somewhere, and she throws back her head as if she is going to charge at him. Her face is contorted in fury and the flesh clings to the bone; it could be a death mask; it is not a human face at all.

"Yes!" she says. "I've never forgiven you. And I never will. You wanted him dead and he is. He's dead. Just as you wanted."

She turns her face from him. She does not want to look at him, but then she feels herself falling on the stairs again, she feels the miscarriage start in her again, and all the stored hatred rises up and she turns back to him and goes on.

"Just as you wanted me dead too. Oh yes, Eugene Henderson Fayer, you haven't fooled me as much as you've thought. I know you. I've become like you."

She is trembling, there is spittle on her lip. She wants to run, but instead she rips the comb from the knot in her hair and crushes it in her hand. The teeth pierce the flesh of her palm, which begins to bleed, but she does not notice. Her hair tumbles around her wild face.

"Well, I'm alive, Eugene. I'm alive and it's you who are dying. And how do you like that!"

She is standing at the foot of his bed, shouting at him. Her knuckles bulge through the skin as she grips the brass rails of his bed. This is not happening, she knows. This is no part of her present. She is going down the stairs to the kitchen. She is pouring the gin into a glass and she is drinking it in huge quick gulps. But this is not happening either.

"I'm alive," she says. Her hair tumbles about her face as she listens to the voice full of hatred and revenge. "I'm alive and it's you who are dying." Her voice.

And then she wakes the next morning and, by some miracle, Eugene is still alive.

But he knows what she has done.

And she knows.

10

Always there are bells ringing. The great bell in the convent tower rings every quarter hour and the Angelus bells ring at six in the morning and at noontime and in the evening. The sound is different; the Angelus bells toll on and on, and the nuns time each part of the prayer to the tolling of the bells, so that at the end the last sound continues to ring in the air forever, and so does their prayer. Sister Veronica has explained all this. But the bells that interest Jessica Connolly most are the bells at Mass when the priest raises the host and the chalice; that is when the nuns all bend their heads forward, their white veils shifting on their shoulders as they lean toward the altar where God is now present in the flesh. There are other bells, bells she knows nothing about, the ones that ring to call the nuns to special duties, to prayer, to dinner. She does not know about them because they ring in the cloister, behind that marvelous door which none of the little girls are ever allowed to enter. Behind that door the nuns sleep and eat and live their secret lives. Only a Sister can enter that door.

Jessica Connolly has been in St. Vincent's since birth. She lives there with thirty other girls, sometimes more and sometimes fewer, and she is happy. People have come to the orphanage at times to choose a little girl for their own, but Jessica has never been chosen. She has never wanted to be chosen. She wants to stay in the convent forever with her friend Ruth and with Sister Veronica. Twice Jessica has been called from the playground to talk to visitors, but still she has never been chosen. Those two times were in the same year, and that was the year Sister Veronica was in charge of adoptions. "No, it is not possible," she said, smiling and smiling. "Jessica would never do. We have others you will love, much prettier ones. No, Jessica would never do."

Jessica she keeps for herself, and for God. And to make up to her for not being chosen, Sister Veronica gives Jessica a doll which she herself had once been given. She has kept it because . . . she does not know why. But it is a beautiful doll, dressed in a white lace dress from the 1800s, and in the doll's hand is a white silk parasol with ruffles. It is Jessica's one great treasure.

But Jessica Connolly is twelve years old now and no longer plays with the doll, which she has put safely away, just as she also has been put safely away. There is no longer any worry someone will adopt her. She is too old, but even if she were not, there is the problem of her nose, broken and not set properly; and she is tall and skinny. She has not yet grown into her body; at this age there is no telling how she will look as a woman. Her eyes are the only indication, wide and green and warm. It is because of Jessica Connolly's eyes that Sister Veronica has chosen her.

Sister Veronica is walking between Jessica and Ruth. A broad path leads up an incline to an iron gate and a huge spreading elm tree. Inside the gate, the path continues; it winds in irregular circles around the hill. The graves on either side of the path are marked with small white slabs of stone. There is always a light breeze on the hill and all the Sisters like to walk there.

The two girls at Sister Veronica's side are excited and awkward; they cannot walk the way Sister Veronica walks. She glides along the path to the cemetery, her feet making no sound as they touch the white gravel. Her hands are in her sleeves, her eyes cast down. She is the model of the perfect nun; the two girls know it and want to be like her. Her voice is very soft and very musical and she thrills them as she talks about the love of God and the need for sacrifice. Surely not any of the Saints, not Saint Teresa, not Saint Mary Magdalen, was ever as exciting as Sister Veronica.

They have reached the gate to the little cemetery and they pause in the shade of the elm tree. For a moment no one says anything. They are there, three of them, beneath the elm tree. The sun makes the leaves a yellow-green, and the white headstones glisten against the hill. Sister Veronica, age forty, and the two little girls: all of them, for this moment, filled with love and innocence.

And then they open the gate and go through. Sister Veronica is preparing them because in a year they will attend the parish high school with children who are not from the orphanage, children who have mothers and fathers the way Ruth used to. Ruth lived at home until she was six, but then there was a fire and she came to live at St. Vincent's. Ruth does not think of mothers and fathers any more. She, like Jessica, is happy with the nuns, and especially with Sister Veronica.

"You girls are my special girls," Sister Veronica says. "I have no fears for you. You will always do what is right and what is good. It may even be that God has chosen one of you for his own. There is no higher calling." Her voice rises and falls as she glides along the path; she could be singing a rich and difficult plain chant. "But you must never be deceived; the life of a Sister is a life of self-denial, a life of suffering. And in that suffering we find our peace. We find happiness. There is no joy like the joy of service." Her voice is hypnotic, warm with love and devotion, and her jaw is firm and determined. "No human love can be perfect on this earth. All love fails in the end. All love ends in death, but we Sisters are spared that death. We are alone. No one needs us. No one wants us. But we have God, and it is God and only God who does not disappoint. Joy! Joy at the end!" she says, triumphant. "Look! Only look!" She gestures to either side of the path. "All of them, no matter how badly they failed on earth, all of them are saints in heaven."

Jessica and Ruth look down the rows of small white gravestones. They walk here every day during recreation and during Rosary, but they have never thought of a saint beneath each stone. They know all the stones by heart, even the oldest, yellowing and cracked, that go back to 1800. And now these dead women are saints, every one of them. Death and sanctity. Jessica and Ruth long to be saints and to lie beneath a stone. But they cannot, yet. And so they walk with Sister Veronica, the tall thin nun who makes music out of words; they walk and wait for the time when they too can make a total sacrifice of their lives to God.

Meanwhile Sister Veronica continues to prepare them for next year and the high school, where children have parents and where there are boys.

It is a year later. Jessica and Ruth are both thirteen now, and freshmen in the parish high school. The school is taught by nuns, but not the nuns at the orphanage school. These nuns wear black. There are no singing classes here and no walks in the middle of the day. No one passes around beautiful books with colored pictures of the saints. The school is huge and cold, with high empty windows that open and close with a pole. There are no little casement windows that crank open like the one in Jessica's cubicle that looks out on a corner of the cloister garden. Jessica does not like this school, but it is her duty to do well, and so she does. Sister Veronica is pleased with her. And Ruth is her friend.

Ruth is pretty and everyone likes her, even the nuns. She has grown tall, almost as tall as Jessica, and her white shirt has begun to stick out in front. Ruth has long dark hair which falls past her shoulders in curls. Her skin is very white and her gray eyes, with their dark lashes, look as if they have been set by mistake in the wrong face. They are mild eyes, passive, and they make Ruth's customary animation seem almost wild. She smiles all the time.

Jessica is proud of her privileged position as Ruth's friend.

Because of Ruth, Jessica is invited to sit with the most popular girls during lunch. And twice she has gone along with Ruth to afternoon tea at homes where there are parents, to the Price's home and to the Kelly's. Jessica is shy, eager to make friends but not knowing how to say the things Ruth says, so that people will like her and want to be with her. This world of conversations at the water fountain and in the cloakroom, this world where girls become friends and then stop being friends, this world confuses her. It frightens her. She is more grateful each day that Ruth, who knows this world and thrives in it, is her own special friend.

St. Vincent's lies outside the town and, since no one lives in their direction, Jessica and Ruth walk together to and from school. They have been doing this for four months, through the warm fall mornings and later through the gray mornings of November and now through the clean white snow.

It is near Christmas. Jessica sees less of Ruth at school these days because Ruth has taken up with Alice Price whose brother Bill is sixteen and handsome. Ruth has told Jessica her secret.

"I love him and when I grow up I'm going to marry him."

"But don't you want to be a nun? What about Sister Veronica?"

"You can be a nun for both of us," Ruth says, laughing, as she tosses her hair. Jessica clutches her books to her chest. She has nothing to say. In this school everything is different; everything is slipping away from her. She is grateful that she still has Sister Veronica.

At St. Vincent's there are special services to prepare for the coming of Christmas. All the girls say an extra Rosary or impose an extra penance on themselves; these are straws for the Christ Child's crib. And on Saturdays they twine laurel into wreaths and long streamers that will hang along the walls of the chapel and on the convent doors. The Sisters let them eat apples while they twine, and afterwards they have hot chocolate and sweets. And each evening there is the beautiful singing. Jessica sits in the chapel on the outside of the grill and watches the choir sisters stand together up near the altar and practice the soaring notes of the Palestrina Mass they will sing at midnight on Christmas and then the carols they will sing around the tree in the recreation room. There is no home like this home. It is God's home and his love is a fire. Sister Veronica's words have never been so important to Jessica as they are now.

At the parish high school there is no singing and no special decorations. Each classroom has a tiny wooden crèche, empty, awaiting Jesus and Mary and Joseph, and that is all. Advent is a time of preparation here, not a time of joy, and the last week before Christmas is given over completely to the annual retreat, so that the students can prepare themselves for the coming of Christ. A Redemptorist Father is giving the retreat and each morning all the children assemble in the auditorium to hear him speak about sin and damnation and the wonderful saving grace of the Lord Jesus Christ. On the third day he begins hearing their confessions.

He hears the boys first. They line up, a class at a time, and, single file, march from the school building across the playground to the church. They are not allowed to get their coats and they make a great show of freezing in the cold winter air. In the church they kneel at the altar rail until Sister taps each one on the shoulder to send him into the confessional booth. And then the next and the next. They remain kneeling at the altar rail until everyone's confession is heard and then they file back to their classrooms, shivering in earnest now, since the church is not heated.

The Redemptorist does not get to the girls until after lunch and the sister in charge has begun to get nervous. She knows that Father wants to finish confessions in one day, but he is patient and thorough, and what can she do? She makes the girls hurry as she leads them from the school to the church.

Jessica's class is the first to be summoned, though she and Ruth will make their confessions last since they are from St.

Vincent's. Ruth has already gone into the booth and Jessica is waiting for the tap on her shoulder. Jessica likes confession. She thanks God that she has never committed a mortal sin, has never sacrificed his love.

In a minute she hears the little window slide shut and at the same time feels a tap on her shoulder. Ruth comes out of the booth, her head bowed and a slight smile on her lips. She holds back the crimson curtain and Jessica slips inside. Just as she kneels, the curtain falls back over the opening, shutting out all light. Finally the little window slides open and she begins her confession.

She has told her sins—negligence in prayer, uncharitable thoughts, lack of generosity—and is waiting for her penance, but there is only silence on the other side of the little screen. And then there is a sigh. The priest says, "And are you one of the girls from St. Vincent's?"

"Yes, Father." She is amazed. How could he know this? She hears him sigh again.

"I see," he says. "And you must be about thirteen or fourteen, child, are you not?"

"Thirteen, Father."

"Thirteen, yes," he says. He is Irish, she can tell by the way he talks; he has a brogue like Mr. Kelly. "Thirteen. And tell me, child, do you know all about life? Do you know about babies and all?"

Jessica says nothing. She knows about menstruation, Sister Veronica has told her, but she doesn't know about babies. She does not want to.

"Do you know where babies come from, child?"

"I think they come from the mother."

"That's right, child. Now, do you know how they get inside the mother?"

Jessica is dizzy. She sways on the kneeler and bumps her forehead against the metal screen. She wants to run, but she cannot move; she knows she must continue with this until the end.

"A woman's body is very specially formed, child. Where

her legs join there is a special place that is hollowed out inside. It's like a lock, you see. And the man's body is specially formed as well." He pauses. "Have you ever seen a man's body, child, without his clothes?"

"No, Father," she says at once, but she has, at least in a picture. It was a picture of a statue in Rome, in a square, and he had a thing hanging there, where there should have been nothing. Jessica had turned the page quickly, but later she had turned back and looked at it carefully. There was something frightening about it, that thing. And now here is a priest talking about it.

"The man's body is formed, my child, the opposite of the woman's. Where she is shaped like a lock, he is shaped like a key. And so these two parts are brought together, in love, like the key in a lock, so that a tiny part of him remains inside her, like a little seed, and from that seed a baby grows. And this is God's holy way of bringing new life into the world." He waits for some kind of response, but the girl says nothing. "Do you understand now, child?"

"Yes, Father."

He hears the strangeness in her voice. "All right now, that's all over with, so tell me, do you think these things are ugly that I've told you? Because they're not, you know; this is God's way. It is all part of his plan. And if some day you're to marry and be a mother, you have to know these things, and know that they're beautiful, not dirty or ugly."

"Yes, Father."

He sighs again. Well, better that she hear it in confession than in some dirty conversation in the girls room. He sniffles. He is coming down with a cold. Damn.

"For your penance, child, say three Hail Marys and a Glory be." He mumbles the words of absolution, gives her a blessing, and she is free.

The little window has rattled shut, but Jessica continues to kneel in the confessional. The window opens again, he is ready for the next penitent, and Jessica pushes away from the kneeler so quickly that she falls against the curtain. Sister is there suddenly, and she pulls the curtain aside and grasps Jessica's arm.

"Well, you certainly took enough of Father's time," she says, and her fingers dig into the soft part of Jessica's arm. But then Sister sees the girl's face, white as ashes, and she pushes her into a pew. "Just sit there," she says. "You mustn't faint. Above all, you mustn't faint." They sit together in the pew while the class files out of the church and the next class files in. Sister breathes deeply into her folded hands. The confessions are going too slowly, the class is going gack to school unattended, and now this girl. Only God knows what she has said in confession, only God knows if she is going to faint. Life is too much sometimes. But in the end Jessica does not faint.

Jessica cannot eat her dinner and she does not sleep that night. The next morning, her forehead is hot and she is dizzy, but she does not tell anyone. It is too horrible, what she knows. At school she decides she will tell Ruth, but she can never get her alone. Ruth is surrounded, always, with girls who are laughing and whispering. But after school Jessica is in luck; they walk together back to St. Vincent's and they are alone.

Ruth's books are tied with a leather strap and she swings the strap back and forth so that the book bindings make funny little tracks in the snow. She is chattering about boys and about Billy, she is saying they will get married when they're grown up.

"He asked me if I had ever seen a man without his clothes on." Jessica's eyes are wide and she gasps as she hears her own voice. So, she has said it.

"Who? Who asked you that?"

"The priest. In confession yesterday."

"He never did." Ruth stops swinging her books and looks intently at Jessica. "What did he say, exactly?"

"He said 'have you ever seen a man without his clothes on.' "

"And what did you say?"

"I said no."

Ruth swings her books by the strap again. The two girls walk along in silence.

"I have. I saw my father once."

Jessica's face has begun to go crimson.

"He was lying on his bed taking a nap and my mother sent me upstairs to wake him because it was time for dinner, and he was lying on his bed with the sheet off, and I saw him." Ruth giggles. "That's how they make love."

Make love. Jessica's heart is pounding. She is terrified. And Ruth goes on, not even noticing.

"I'll tell you a secret. I've *felt* one, too."

"Ruth!"

"I have. Well, not with my hand, but I felt it up against me. Sometimes, when I go to the Price's and we're up in the nursery, Alice will go out of the room and Billy and I kiss and hug, and right away he gets all hard down there, and I can feel it against me."

Jessica can say nothing.

"And it feels warm and I feel all sort of sleepy and . . ."

"That's a mortal sin, Ruth. You'll go to hell."

"Don't be silly, Jessie. It's nice. It makes me feel good." She thinks for a minute. "Maybe it would be a sin for you, but it's not for me."

Ruth goes on talking, but Jessica does not listen. Jessica is praying that none of this will ever happen to her.

"You won't tell on me, Jessie. Promise."

"I promise."

"You're my best friend," Ruth says, and they walk back to St. Vincent's hand in hand.

Again Jessica cannot eat her dinner, and afterwards, when all the children go to the recreation room to play games, she asks permission to go to chapel instead. She kneels behind the grill and prays that she will never grow up. She does not want blood to come out of her the way Sister Veronica has said it will. She does not want a man to take off his clothes and come inside her and leave part of himself there. She does not want a body at all. "Please, please," she whispers in the darkened chapel. The sanctuary lamp throws a red glare on the crucifix suspended over the altar. Christ's body is bathed in the red light. He is covered with blood, she thinks. But of course he was God, he wouldn't have one of those things. But maybe he did. She looks again at the crucifix and, as she watches, the white cloth about his waist falls away and he is naked before her and, yes, he does. Even he. Jessica buries her face in her hands, crying, until at last someone finds her and takes her to the infirmary.

Sister Veronica sits by her bed, sewing, as the bell in the tower rings midnight. She has said nothing to Jessica for the past three hours, thinking that when it is time, the girl will confide in her. But now it is midnight and she cannot wait any longer.

"Tell me, Jessie," Sister Veronica says. "It always helps to talk about things."

There is a long moment of silence and then Jessica Connolly cannot bear the awful knowledge any longer. "He asked me if I had seen a man without his clothes on. He told me about babies." She throws herself out of the high infirmary bed and clutches Sister Veronica's knees, burying her face in that clean white cloth.

Sister Veronica listens, understanding, while Jessica pours out the story of the priest in confession, of the terrible things he has said. Sister runs her long white hand over the sobbing girl's hair, her chosen one, her child of grace, and then at last Jessica grows quiet.

Through the dark window Sister Veronica can see that it has begun to snow again. Tomorrow the world will be white.

"In time, Jessica, with the passage of years, you may look back and realize that this is all part of the mysterious workings of grace. God chooses us, we do not choose him. Your reaction to what Father has told you may be merely a sign of great joy ahead, a sign that God has chosen you to love *him* only, not any man, not any other person on earth. There is no joy like that joy."

Sister Veronica talks on and on, of God's love, of his mercy, of the mysterious workings of grace.

In the great tower the bell rings once. Sister Veronica places her palm on the little girl's forehead. It is cooler now, she will be able to sleep.

Sister Veronica is gone, but Jessica Connolly does not sleep. She is sitting in the chair by the window looking out at the falling snow. The flakes are tiny and they drift slowly to the ground. Though there is no moon, she can see everything perfectly. It looks warm outside in the soft snow, but it is cold inside and she has wrapped herself in a blanket. Her breath makes frost on the window pane.

Jessica is not thinking of what Sister Veronica has said. She has forgotten it; it is like a piece of music; she cannot remember the words, only the notes rising and falling, the beautiful voice moving effortlessly from passage to passage.

She is looking down on the high walled garden. The dark bushes are only mounds of white now and the garden walks have all disappeared. The pointed arches of the cloister frame the garden in black and white. She sees herself, in a long white habit, her hands folded in her sleeves. She is walking along the garden path, her head bent, her white habit invisible against the white snow. Snow is falling and her whole world is being transformed.

Suddenly she is flooded with warmth, with relief. She will be free. She will be a nun.

11

Sister Judith, who has not been Jessica Connolly for over ten years now, has come into the room just in time. The doctor has been paged by heart emergency and so he drops the penis and the catheter and says to Sister Judith, "Here, you finish this." She pulls back the curtain surrounding the bed to see what it is she must finish. "Yes, doctor," she says, and puts down the tray she is carrying.

The penis has been dilated and the red rubber tube is already in the meatus. She takes the penis firmly in her left hand and pulls; with her right hand she eases the tube gently upward. The patient winces and she stops for a moment. "I know," she says, "it's very painful." Her voice is soft and cool and she goes on talking, not looking at him, while she eases the long length of tube through his penis and into the bladder. "It's just one of those things that has to be done."

Sister Judith does all those things that have to be done. She is the perfect nun, the perfect nurse. She is professional. The penis into which she is inserting the tube is large, uncircumsized. She barely notices. It is simply another part of the body that needs caring for.

The tube is inserted, the urine will flow drop by drop into the bottle under the bed. Sister Judith has not yet looked at the patient's face and she does not now. "The pain will go in a short while," she says, pulling the white curtain back from the bed. "You'll feel better." She takes her tray which holds a bowl of sudsy water and a razor and she goes to the other bed. "This won't hurt at all," she says, and draws the curtains around. She is going to prepare him for an appendectomy.

Sister Judith's life is a life of care for others. She knows that it is not her they need; anyone could do the things she does for them. Nor do they want her especially; she is anonymous; she is a nun. But she can do these things, and so she must. She gives baths and empties bedpans, she hands instruments to doctors who cut the body open and hack away at the insides, and when she must, she pumps stomachs or inserts catheters. There is nothing she cannot do.

Later, when she brings orange juice from bed to bed, Sister Judith checks the catheter patient to see if the urine is flowing as it should. A glance at the bottle tells her that it is; she checks the bottle so swiftly that he fails to notice what she is doing, even though he is studying her, fascinated. She smiles at him, a warm but impersonal smile, and hands him his orange juice.

He is looking at her in a special way, trying to catch her eye, as if they are in collusion about something. She does not respond. He can still feel her cool hand on him as she shoved in that rubber tube.

"*Nil alienum mihi,*" he says, shaking his head.

"Pardon me?"

"I said *nil alienum mihi.* Terence. *Humanus sum; nil humanum me alienum puto,* to be exact."

"Oh," she says.

"Don't you know Latin? I thought all nuns studied Latin."

" 'I'm human,' " she says. "I got that much, but I didn't get the last part."

"I am human. And so nothing that concerns any human can be foreign to me."

"I'm not very good at Latin."

She smiles.

He has never seen such green eyes.

But she has missed the point. He is complimenting her, partly, and partly he is reminding her where she has just put that tube. But she does not see. Or she chooses not to see. He looks at her, calculating, while she looks back, expecting some explanation.

"I meant you have to do a lot of dirty work as a nun."

"Oh, none of it is dirty. Not when people are in pain."

"Well, that's what I meant. *Nil alienum mihi.*"

Sister Judith turns to go and he stops her.

"My name is Eugene Fayer."

"Yes, I know. Your chart," and she indicates his medical chart which hangs on a hook at the foot of his bed. "Eugene Henderson Fayer," she says. "Roman Catholic. No priest desired."

He ignores her remark about the priest. But she is sharp. She has put him in his place with three words.

"And may I know your name, Sister?"

"I'm Sister Judith."

"Sister Judith."

"Yes."

"Sister Judith, who fears not man nor beast."

"I must go," she says, and in a moment she has given the other patient his orange juice and a smile and she is gone.

Sister Judith goes from room to room, from bed to bed, cool and unruffled, and her heart is beating faster, faster. But why? Is it what he has said? Is it the way he looked at her? Or is it the tone he took—Sister Judith, who fears not man nor beast—what can that mean? She puts the matter out of her mind, she does her work, she prays. But at night she cannot sleep; she turns over and over on her tongue the words *humanus sum; nil alienum mihi.*

The next day and the day after she manages to have some other sister bring Eugene Fayer his meals and check his bottle. By the third day she has forgotten him, or at least he has become unimportant to her. She brings him breakfast herself.

"You're back, Sister Judith," he says. "I was afraid you had moved to another floor . . . or run away."

"We've been very busy," she says, glancing beneath the bed to check the bottle. It is gone. So, he is off catheter. She studies his chart for a moment, saying mechanically, "Enjoy your breakfast," but as she says it she looks up from the chart and sees that he is smiling at her. He smiles, letting his lips slip away very slowly so that his teeth seem somehow exposed, naked. They are unnaturally white. His lower lip is thick and wet looking. Sister Judith fees her heart jump and, because he continues to look at her this way, she looks at his chart again and frowns. "Very good," she says and, with her eyes lowered, goes to the other bed.

She checks the chart of the patient with the appendectomy. There has been some problem, he is not recovering as he should. She looks at his eyes, places one hand on his forehead; he is burning. She tosses back the covers and checks the dressing on his incision; at once she turns away from the ripe smell of pus. Eugene Fayer is saying something to her, but she does not listen, he is forgotten. This patient needs attention; he needs a doctor. She walks swiftly from the room, her skirts rustling as she goes, and Eugene, who has still not touched his breakfast, watches her. There will be another time.

In the evening, after night prayers, Sister Judith goes directly to bed. Usually she meditates for an hour, turning over in her mind the good things that have happened during the day and thanking God for them, but tonight she is exhausted. She does not want to think. She wants to be unconscious.

But she cannot sleep. She lays in her narrow bed trying to make her mind a blank, but stray thoughts come to her anyway. An hour passes and then another. She is disoriented; the ceiling seems to be pressing down upon her and the bed floats. Perhaps she has a fever. When finally she hears the clock strike one, she gets out of bed and puts on her bathrobe.

Sister Judith crouches at her kneeler, praying. "I want to love you, I want to love you," she whispers to the crucifix clutched between her folded hands. "I want only to love you and serve you."

Then what is wrong? Just do it, she thinks to herself, but she finds herself saying with even more urgency, "I want to, oh I want to." This has happened before, this desperation, but always she has been able to lose it in work. She has volunteered to clean the toilets, to launder the older sisters' habits with their yards and yards of heavy serge, she has worked and prayed.

She feels heavy; her limbs are made of lead and they ache at every joint. It hurts her just to kneel. "I want to love you," and she pushes herself up from the kneeler and opens the door to the corridor. At this hour it is lit by only one small bulb. It is a dark tunnel at one end; pale moonlight filters through the small circular window at the other.

She walks softly, softly, in her soft white slippers down the corridor of the convent dormitory. Everyone is asleep. Only Sister Judith, she thinks, only crazy Judith paces the black corridor in the middle of the night. "Oh God in heaven, help me," she whispers, her knuckles growing white around the crucifix, which she presses to her mouth. "I want to love you. I want to."

She is dizzy, she stumbles, and then supports herself for a moment against the wall. She is at the far end of the corridor in the blackness, and she looks down the long hall to the tiny light in the middle; more blackness stretches beyond that. Is it her life she is looking at? Where do these thoughts come from? Is she going mad? Sisters do go mad, she knows, she has taken care of them. Things happen to them, things affect their minds. Look at Sister Veronica.

She must not think of that, she must make her mind a blank. She clenches her teeth and forces all thought from her brain and yet the words go on, "I want to love and serve you."

Sister Judith has walked toward the light in the corridor and now she has moved beyond it. She is approaching the little circular window at the far end of the corridor where there is a patch of moonlight on the floor. She stands at the window.

"I want to love you," she says.

It is almost two o'clock. The streets are deserted, there is not a sound outside, not a sound in the house. Sister Judith feels the long black corridor at her back and the soft moonlight through the little window. She grows less desperate as she gazes as far as she can see in one direction and then in the other. It is quiet out there, peaceful. The words in her brain begin to slow down and she becomes aware of the pain where she has driven the corpus of the crucifix into her palm. She shifts the cross to the other hand, staring still at the deserted street.

And then she sees something move on the dark sidewalk. A couple, a young boy and girl not more than seventeen, are walking with their arms around each other. They are in front of the Good Value Grocery and they pause in the little circle of light thrown by the nightlamp. He puts his arms around her waist and she arches toward him, encircling his neck with her arms. They move slowly, gently, into a kiss and then after a moment they move apart. He puts one arm around her waist as they walk slowly out of the patch of light and disappear once more into the darkness.

Sister Judith is smiling. Everything is so peaceful in the street, everything is so calm. She raises the crucifix to her breast, still standing at the window, not moving.

I am at peace here, she thinks, this is where I belong. The desperation of the last hours falls from her completely and she is flooded with the warm assurance that she is here, she is home, she wants only to love God.

"I want you to love me," she says and begins to repeat it when she realizes suddenly what she has said. "I want to love you," she corrects herself. She is embarrassed at her stupidity—to ask for love. "But yes," she says. "That *is* what I want. I exist too, and I want to be loved." She does not believe she is saying these things, and to God!

But the words fill her with a strange kind of power. They are honest, they are the truth. It is right to say them. "I want you to love me," she says softly, "I want to be loved." Her tone is urgent. Whatsoever you ask the Father in my name shall be given unto you. "Well, I want to be loved."

She turns and walks from the window, firmly now, confident that she has accomplished something, or rather that some marvelous thing has been accomplished in her. She will have God's love because she has asked for it. The kingdom of heaven is taken by force and the violent bear it away.

Sister Judith has no trouble falling asleep now. She is dead to the world before she has finished saying the Magnificat.

Sister Judith is up at five, refreshed, eager to begin a day of hard work. It is Thursday, her day off from the hospital, and she will spend it at St. Vincent's with Sister Veronica and with little Jessie Price. Sister Veronica is fifty-eight and everyone expects her to die soon. She has suffered enough, God knows.

Nine years earlier, as Jessica Connolly was pronouncing her vows of poverty, chastity, and obedience, Sister Veronica experienced a sharp pain in her left temple. She paid no attention to it, even though it forced tears from her eyes, nor did she pay any attention later to the lightheadedness she felt, nor to the pain in her chest. Jessica's becoming a Sister, *her* Sister, was after all the fulfillment of a dream. What did a blinding flash in the temple signify, or a small stabbing pain in the heart? But at dinner she had trouble with her speech and once, when she reached for her glass of water, it was several inches from where she tried to close her hand upon it. Thrombosis? No. Impossible. She was a young woman in the full vigor of life, forty-nine, and never sick for a day. She went to her room to lie down and by morning the damage had been done.

"She's had a C.V.A.," the doctor said, "cerebral apoplexy." It was not immediately clear how much brain damage there was.

And so, for the past nine years Sister Veronica has been fed her meals, helped in and out of bed, and when the weather allows she has been put out in her wheelchair to enjoy the sun. The Sisters read to her or sit beside her saying the Rosary aloud, hoping that one day she will respond. Lately, in fact, she has shown signs of some returning mental activity. While one of the novices was reading to her from the *Imitation of Christ,* she became very agitated and her right hand flailed from side to side as if she were trying to catch something that kept slipping from her grasp. And more recently, while Sister Judith was talking to her, her face tightened in terrible concentration as she tried to say something, but no words came out, and in a moment her mouth went slack again and her eyes blank. Nine years of silence for that soaring hypnotic voice; Sister Judith thinks of it and tears come to her eyes. Death will be a kind deliverer after all.

It is a beautiful day and Sister Judith wheels the heavy wood and metal chair through the cloister walks of the walled garden, talking all the while to Sister Veronica, soothing her with her voice, reassuring her she is loved. Sister Judith is thinking of that day, how long ago, when she and Ruth walked on either side of Sister Veronica up the white gravel incline to the cemetery. Sister Veronica had talked to them about . . . what? About suffering. About happiness. Yes, that was it. "His love is a fire," she had said. "Joy! Joy at the end!" They had stood for just a moment beneath the branches of the elm tree and they were together. And now Ruth is dead, and her daughter Jessie is at St. Vincent's, and Sister Veronica is waiting, waiting. Sister Judith wants to confide in Sister Veronica; she wants to tell her about last night, about her revelation. I want you to love me, she thinks, and as the words turn over in her mind she feels again that surge of power.

Yes, it is right, it is true.

"Sister?" she says, kneeling before the wheelchair. But it is hopeless. Sister Veronica's head lolls to the side and a long string of spittle slips from her mouth. Sister Judith catches it in her handkerchief and then wipes Sister's mouth. "Poor sweet," she says. "You should have a handkerchief with you all the time." She fumbles in the pockets concealed in the heavy folds of Sister Veronica's habit and she brings out a gleaming white handkerchief, a small linen square with three tiny strawberries embroidered in the corner. "There," she says, "you can keep that in your hand for when you need it," and watches as Sister Veronica's hand closes on it, the fingers contracting like a claw.

"Come on," she says, to hide her tears at the wreckage of this woman, this saint, "come on, I'll see if I can find Jessie and we can take our old walk. Would you like that?" But of course there is no response. "I think you will. It's a lovely day for it."

But there is no need to look for Jessie; she is sitting on the steps outside the cloister garden. Jessie Price is twelve years old and the image of her mother. She is tall for her age and she has long dark hair which falls past her shoulders in curls. Her skin is very white and her gray eyes are set off by long dark lashes. She is somber and the sisters admire her for her gravity and for her remarkable intelligence. She almost never smiles.

"Jessie, dear. How lucky we are to find you. Would you like to walk with Sister Veronica and me?" Sister Judith kneels again beside the wheelchair. "You remember Ruth Price's daughter, don't you, Sister? Jessie Price? Isn't she the picture of Ruth?"

Sister Veronica focuses for a minute and then she shakes her head from side to side. Jessie Price smiles at Sister Veronica because she knows that will please Sister Judith.

"May I?" Jessie says, and takes Sister Judith's place behind the chair. That way the two sisters can talk.

"Do you remember, Sister, when Ruth and I were girls, how you were so good to us? You used to talk about God and the religious life, a life of service, and you were the whole world to us. You *gave* us our world. You'll never know how completely you influenced us on those walks, talking to us with your marvelous voice. We were hypnotized. We were transported."

Sister Judith smiles, thinking of the perfection of those days. They were young then. Sister Veronica was tall and beautiful and glided along the white gravel path. Ruth was safe still, and she herself . . . well, she was the same as she is. Jessica Connolly and Sister Judith are one. She has never changed. She has only worked harder, prayed more, tried to give whatever was asked and whatever could be given. She has tried to love God. She loves him. And now, for the first time, she is asking to be loved by him. The daring of it

They are at the tree and the iron gate. Sister Veronica and Sister Judith and Ruth's daughter Jessie pause for a moment beneath the shade of the elm. Silent, they watch the gravestones glistening white against the green grass. The circle is complete: the three of them resting at the cemetery gate.

"Jessie, go on ahead a little, while I have a word with Sister."

And Jessie goes, somber under the burden of her mother's sins. But none of that matters anymore, she knows, because now she has Sister Judith for a mother. Jessie touches the doll's parasol, white silk with ruffles, that she carries, always, in the pocket of her uniform. It was Sister Judith's first gift to her; it is a treasure, it is a pledge.

Jessie walks away from them as Sister Judith kneels again before the wheelchair and clasps Sister Veronica's folded hands between her own.

"Sister, I must tell you," she begins, and then stops because she has no words for what has happened. "I had a . . . something . . . happen to me last night, late. I couldn't sleep and I got up to pray. I was at the kneeler, praying, and it got worse, the feeling of being lost and desperate and I wanted just to love God more fully, more completely, and I went out into the corridor, it was pitch black, and I walked up and down, praying. And then suddenly I found myself saying words that I had been saying over and over but now they were different. I was saying, "I want to be loved," and "I want *you* to love *me*." And I thought, that's blasphemy, but in a second it came to me that, no, that is what God wants too. That is God's way. And I felt, oh, I can't tell you how I felt."

Sister Judith has been talking rapidly, the words tumbling upon one another as she whispers them into her hands, which clutch the lifeless hands of Sister Veronica. "I can't tell you how I felt," she says, her voice filled with joy. She kneels up straight and tosses back her head so that she looks Sister Veronica full in the face.

Sister Veronica's cheeks are wet with tears and her face is contorted with the effort of trying to speak. Her lips move, but there is no sound.

"I didn't mean," Sister Judith says, "oh, please, you mustn't cry. I wanted to make you happy. I wanted to tell you."

"Leave." Sister Veronica's voice is harsh and guttural. It is as if she is speaking from some other world.

Sister Judith pulls away from her, her green eyes large with surprise. What does this mean? Why is she crying?

"Leave," Sister Veronica says, her voice trailing off to a whisper so that the rest of what she says is lost. Her eyes cease focusing and her jaw goes slack, but as Sister Judith continues to kneel before her in astonishment, she hears the voice say clearly—there is no question about the words—"Leave the convent."

"What?" she asks. "What do you mean? What did you say?"

But Sister Veronica cannot answer; she slumps to the side, still alive, still waiting.

Sister Judith kneels by the wheelchair until Jessie Price joins them. In silence they go back down the path to the convent, three women with their hearts full.

• • •

Mrs. Fayer is sitting on the green bench in Louisburg Square. She has gathered her torn pictures, her holy cards with prayers on the back, her scattered possessions. She has stuffed them into her purse, all except the photograph of Sister Veronica. The picture has been torn across the nose; only the broad forehead and intense eyes remain. A border of black runs around the edge of the little card and on the back there is some printing. "Sister Veronica Mary Mercer, 1872–1970. In the Cross is Salvation."

"May God have mercy on her," she says.

Mrs. Fayer is in the present on a green bench in Louisburg Square because for her there is no past, but in this present she is Sister Judith and she is walking the gravel path that leads to the cemetery. Ruth's daughter Jessie is at her side. Jessie Price is only eight years old, but she is intelligent and solemn.

"You're very special to me, Jessie, and you're very special to God." Sister Judith talks on and on in her rich musical voice, and the little girl listens, fascinated. "His love is the only love that matters," she says, "because his love is eternal. All human loves end in death."

Sister Judith glides along the path, her feet soundless on the white gravel. Her hands are in her sleeves, her eyes cast down.

Two years have passed. "God is love," she says, "and his love is a fire that in the end will burn away our every imperfection. In the end even our virtues do not matter. God is the only thing that matters. Not all our works, not any of our suffering. Him only and forever." And Jessie Price nods gravely.

Two more years pass and it is the present. Jessie Price sits on the steps outside the cloister hoping that Sister Judith will come out and walk with her. And she does. Jessie pushes Sister Veronica's wheelchair up the hill to the cemetery while Sister Judith walks beside the older nun, talking. When they get to the tree and the iron gate, Sister Judith sends her on ahead. She leaves the two nuns alone, angry that she is excluded, but smiling at Sister Veronica because that will please Sister Judith. When she comes back, she sees that Sister Judith has been crying. Good. They are even now. The three of them come slowly down the hill to the convent.

It is the last time Jessie Price sees Sister Judith. When they next meet, the little girl will be a stout woman of fifty, Doctor Jessie Price, or Mrs. Price as she chooses to call herself. And Sister Judith? For Jessie, Sister Judith will be gone forever within the month.

Mrs. Fayer, on her green bench in Louisburg Square, gives the picture one final look and then she puts it into her purse. Sister Veronica. Jessie Price. What does any of it mean?

There is a small breeze that lasts only for a moment, but the leaves flutter and the grass at her feet is dappled suddenly with patches of light. Mrs. Fayer shuts her eyes and the world around her is transformed. She thinks she begins to see something, to understand.

A powerful motor roars somewhere in the distance. She shakes her head. Poor Adam, she thinks, poor Martha.

But her thoughts drift back to Sister Veronica, who has died, finally, at ninety-eight. Those endless years of suffering.

And Jessie Price, dead for three years now.

How, then, can Mrs. Fayer have seen her only today?

She smiles, because she is alive and because she knows that anything is possible.

• • •

Sister Judith has been to St. Vincent's to visit Sister Veronica, who has said to her, "Leave," and now it is the next day and she is at work in the hospital. The man with the appendectomy has died, even though this is 1930 and almost nobody dies from appendectomies anymore. Eugene Fayer has the room to himself. His leg is healing well after his operation; he will walk with only a slight limp. He sits up much of the day now, but he is not allowed to walk on the leg. He is watching Sister Judith arrange his tray for lunch.

"Jessica," he says.

She looks up sharply.

"Jessica Connolly."

She frowns, pained for some reason.

"I've been asking the night nurse about you," he says. "Jessica Connolly, who fears not man nor beast."

"My name," she says coldly, "is Sister Judith."

"Of course," he says, "I was only trying to be friendly." Before she can turn to go, he adds, "My wife has died."

"I'm sorry." Her eyes go soft again.

"Only this month. It was sudden, a heart attack."

"Sometimes it's God's mercy that they die suddenly." She is thinking of Sister Veronica. I want to be loved, she thinks.

"And then my operation. And my lungs. I've had to close the rest home. It's been my month, all right," he says.

"Do you want to talk about it?" This is her work; this is her duty.

"I want to talk to you."

She pretends she does not hear the emphasis on *you*. She sits down to listen.

"Where to begin? She was a nurse, much older than me. We got married after the war. I was even worse then than I am now. My lungs were completely gone and I had to use crutches to walk. She was my nurse, actually."

"Were you married long?"

"Ten years."

"Ten years. I'm sorry . . . that she's passed on, I mean."

"Oh, it's not like that. It wasn't a good marriage, to tell you the truth." He pauses. Does he have her hooked well enough for this? What does he have to lose? "I wasn't always faithful to her. Once I recovered enough to get around freely, I . . . well, you wouldn't know about that, safe in your cloister." For a moment there is bitterness in his voice, but he goes on quickly and his tone changes. "So, where am I? We're married, we have no children; I guess the old people in the home are our children. Or were."

"What were you doing in an old people's home?"

"I wasn't. I was in the vet's hospital."

"But you said she had been your nurse."

"Oh, I see. Yes, she'd been my nurse in the vet's hospital, but when we married, we bought the home. She had some money and I had my disability pension, so we bought the home. It was already a rest home; we just took over the business . . . Is this boring you?"

"No, no. You were saying about the old people."

"You're sure?"

"Go on, please," she says.

"The old people. We had five of them, all old ladies. I had to send them home, back to their children, you know, once she died. My wife, I mean. All except one, and she had nobody, so we put her in the state home." He is silent for a minute. "So I had to close the house. I couldn't handle it alone."

"Yes," Sister Judith says. "It would be too much for a man by himself."

"Well, it's because you've got to have a nurse, you see. It's state law. I'll have to marry another nurse." He smiles that slow smile and his lips pull back, exposing his white teeth, naked. "I should marry you, Sister Judith."

He sees her go white.

"I'm joking, Sister. I didn't mean to offend."

"No," she says. "I know." But she leaves him now, anyway. He smiles to himself, his slow smile, practicing.

It is the next day and they have been talking for almost an hour. Eugene Fayer has made Sister Judith laugh with his stories about the absurdities of life in the army. She is thinking that other patients need her, she should not spend so much time with Mr. Fayer, but she has obviously cheered him up and that is all to the good. She begins to make those motions she always makes just before she goes.

"The army's a lot like the religious life," he says, determined now to keep her here.

"The army!"

"Well," he says, "the discipline, the obedience. *Blind* obedience."

"The discipline, perhaps. But the obedience is different. We obey because we choose to; in the army there is no choice."

"And in the army there's no poverty," he says, agreeing with her. "There's no chastity."

"No." She does not like the way he smiled as he said, "There's no chastity." They sit silent for a moment. She is once again about to leave.

"I was in religion once," he says. "It was before the war."

"Diocesan? Or were you in an order?" She is astonished, but she betrays nothing.

"Aren't you surprised?"

"Should I be surprised?"

He laughs. She is fencing with him; he has made progress.

"Well, I would hope you'd be a little bit surprised."

"Well, I am a little bit surprised."

He has a cane and he leans his chin on the crook and smiles frankly into her face. He has a handsome mouth and a strong chin. Sister Judith tells him she really must go, and she does, gliding soundlessly in her heavy skirts.

Her prayer that night is that she love and serve God better; she does not ask to be loved in return.

It is midafternoon. All morning Sister Judith has been looking forward to this time and now that it has come she has a dull ache at her heart. She does not know why. She is depressed, languid.

"You never did say what kind of seminarian you were," she says. "Diocesan or an order?"

"Diocesan."

"Were you in long? If that isn't too personal."

"Two years. Just short of two years."

"Two years." She has been a nun for . . . how many years? She has been a nun all her life. She is thirty and she has never known any other kind of life. And this man, who has been in religion, has been shot and gassed, has been married and unfaithful, this man is talking to her as if she were . . . what? . . . real. "Two years can be a long time," she says.

"Two days can be a long time, if they're the right two days."

They are silent, thinking.

Sister Judith looks at him: he is scarcely older than she and yet he has lived a whole life. And he is handsome. She leans back against the chair and studies his heavy lips, his strong chin. She closes her eyes, because suddenly in her mind she is kneeling before him, her arms slipping around his waist, while she lowers her head to kiss his chest. She can feel dark hairs beneath the cotton nightgown. She kisses his neck, his collar bone. Below, she can feel him begin to stiffen. She wants to touch him. No, this cannot be happening. This has never happened, this is some terrible dream. I will not surrender to this, she thinks, not hearing what he says.

"Are you all right, Sister? Here, drink this."

Sister Judith drinks the water, both hands around the glass. It is his glass. He has a hand on her shoulder.

"You went dead white; I thought you were going to faint."

"No," she says. "It's only that, I don't know, everything went cloudy for a moment. Thank you," she says. "I'm so terribly sorry. I'm sorry."

Sister Judith is in chapel now whenever she is not on duty. Her back stiff, her hands folded gently on the kneeler, she prays against despair. "Do not abandon me, O Lord, forever," she whispers in the dark. "Do not turn your face from your servant." Her thoughts drift and she finds herself wondering if she is mad. She must lose herself completely in God; it is only in him that our lives have any meaning. She prays and she keeps away from Eugene Fayer.

And then one day, having no intention of doing so, she goes into his room, and sits, and asks him immediately, "Why did you leave?"

"The seminary?"

"Yes."

"Why do you want to know?"

"Because . . . because I care."

"About me?"

"About vocations. About why someone would turn back from the plow once he had set his hand to it."

He smiles. "Rhetoric," he says.

"I'm sorry, Mr. Fayer. I shouldn't have."

"Eugene. Not Mr. Fayer."

"I can't."

"Well, if you can ask me a question like why I left the seminary, you can certainly call me by my name."

"Eugene," she says, pronouncing each syllable separately.

Eugene Fayer studies this woman. He has been amusing himself with her, as he does with all women, but he is angered by her now. She is innocent beyond belief, and yet she has handled his prick, stuck a tube up it, and never blinked an eye. It is her innocence that confounds him. He thinks again, as he always does, of that innocent French girl, that peasant, who threw her arms around him and kissed him because he was an American, because now the Germans had left her village. She had been surprised when he started to pull at her clothes. She fought him, scoring his neck with her fingernails, trying to get at his face. He knocked her unconscious with one blow and then undressed her and raped her with a ferocity that surprised even himself. She was a virgin and afterward her blood was on Eugene and on the kitchen floor where he had laid her. In his mind, it was her innocence that had maddened him; he did not know why. And now this other woman, this Sister Judith, with her innocence that cannot be real. It must be a trick. She's one of those women who are sugary sweet but dangerous underneath. He's seen them before. They're willing to die for an ideal and they're also willing to kill for it. Why should he let her off easy?

"Eugene," she says again.

"All right," he says. "Let me see. I left because of the war; I thought I should be fighting for my country."

"No," she says.

"No. I left because, oh, I left for any number of reasons, I suppose, but basically because of a realization I had one day after a class in moral theology. The priest had been lecturing on ultimate evil—priests love to speculate on that sort of stuff—and he said that the ultimate evil was to use a person as if he were a thing. To dehumanize. He wasn't talking about slavery; he was talking about everyday living. Making a person into a thing. Well, I thought about that for the whole day; it bothered me and I couldn't figure out why. And then that night I was lying in bed and it came to me. If what he said is true then the most evil person that exists is God."

"No," she says, pulling away from him.

"Let me finish. So I decided that the most evil person that exists is God, because we're constantly told that he's infinite and all powerful and eternal and that he needs nothing. He certainly doesn't need us. But he's willing to *use* us, to make us his "instruments." Isn't that what they always say? But we're not necessary to him, not as human beings we're not. Well, right away it occurred to me that something was wrong somewhere. Either the priest was wrong about ultimate evil or all the books are wrong about how God looks at us. And right then and there it came to me that it didn't matter which was wrong, because I didn't want to be used, period. I wanted to be happy. And so I got out."

"To be happy."

"I know. I know. It sounds selfish to you, with your hand to the plow and your perpetual smile, but life is very very short, especially if you're crippled and your lungs are burnt out and you're only thirty-five. If you don't try to make yourself happy, you can be damned sure nobody else will."

To be happy; this is why he left the seminary. Sitting there, opposite this white and trembling nun, he almost believes what he is saying. A man *could* leave religion for this reason. He does not mention what he knows is the real reason: that he walked with his friend in the orchard, talking about the love of God and then about love, and then finally, as it grew dark, he and his friend stepped beneath the heavy branches and exchanged a single soft kiss on the lips. Two men, kissing. The next day he left the seminary and within a week he was in the army. He does not mention this. He does not mention that that same soft kiss still wakes him in the night, in horror, his hands over his face. He mentions only that he is crippled and he has a need to be happy.

"And are you happy?" she says.

"I could be," he says.

Days go by and they continue to talk, but their talk is different now. It is lovers' talk, though they are careful never to mention the word love. Eugene has only been amusing himself with this woman, this Sister Judith, he has meant no real harm. And now he finds that she is different from what he thought. She is not only innocent, she is reluctant, she is passionate in her need to serve God. It amazes him that he has still not been able to break through to her, to make her want him. But he can break through, he is sure of that, and he will.

"Marry me," he says. "Accept me."

"Marry!" At first she is tempted to laugh. How could such a word be spoken to her? She, Jessica Connolly, marry? But in a day or two, marriage does not seem so preposterous. But what would marriage to Eugene be like? She has come to know him well, she thinks, though she knows him only a little. But even that little has shown her he is difficult. The more they talk, the more he changes, as if her love were a burden to him, as if he loved her only while she had been a challenge. She does not understand this, she does not let herself think about it.

Eugene is walking without a cane now, but he is surly and complains about everything. "I can be a roaring bastard," he has said to her. "You have no idea how cruel I can be." And then he smiles that long slow smile. Only at odd moments does he return to his old self, almost shy and diffident, the self Sister Judith has fallen in love with. Then he is whimsical and funny.

Sister Judith prays for guidance.

"Marry me," he says. "I need you," and his voice aches.

But this is impossible, to make such a choice. Sister Judith has never made any choice, except to serve.

But to be loved? To be happy?

"Jessica," he says. "I need you."

Within a week Eugene Fayer is discharged from the hospital and within another he is married to Jessica Connolly, who used to be Sister Judith and who will never be the same again.

12

Jessica is in Amherst, standing forever at the parlor window. The weight she put on during her two years of drinking has begun to fall away. She looks healthy now, even pretty. Dr. Turner has begun calling on her more often than necessary and staying longer than he ought, but she has not noticed, caught up as she is in her present. She is thirty-five and she has lost her child and now her husband.

It is summer, 1935, and hot already, even though the sun has not yet risen. A few birds have begun to make morning noises in the bushes, but they are early. There is still another hour of darkness yet.

Jessica lifts her cigarette to her lips and inhales deeply. The smoke burns her lungs and satisfies her; it is her consolation for not drinking. She has not had a drink for two months now, not since Eugene left, not since she first realized the truth of what he said: she is trying to destroy herself by destroying him.

Jessica inhales again, deeply, and lets the smoke curl from her nostrils in thin gray wisps. How many mornings of how many years stretch ahead of her, old at thirty-five, a reformed drunk? How many? She watches as the smoke touches the window pane and diffuses, going from gray to white and disappearing finally into the air.

Across the road, the steep hill and the meadow lie concealed in darkness. She saw three deer there once—was it only two years ago? A buck and two does grazing, the buck's antlers black and silver in the moonlight.

And so she is going up the stairs to Virgil's room above the garage. He is lying on his back, she is on top, grinding him deeper into herself. This will never end. And now he carries her through the house; both of them are naked and laughing, their black and white limbs mingle. Yes, this is the present and she lives it and lives it.

What has she made of her life? What has she become? The walled garden, the gravel path to the cemetery, Sister Veronica, the long years as a nurse: gone, all of them. Jessica stands at the window, smoking, and she sees herself reflected in the window pane—her left arm clutching her waist, her right tipped out from her body, a cigarette burning in her fingers—and she knows that the walled garden and Sister Veronica could never have happened to her. Those days and nights of prayer, those years of dedication belong to someone else, to Sister Judith. And yet she *must* be Sister Judith.

Jessica cannot understand this. Whatever Sister Judith did made sense; her prayers, her work belonged to *her,* to that other woman who was good and who was young even at thirty, and who was happy. But that Sister Judith has been transformed, like the woman in the myth who was pursued by some god and who cried out for help and was changed into a laurel tree. But Jessica does not feel changed; she feels dead; she feels nothing. She is not Sister Judith any longer. Well then, who is she?

Mrs. Fayer, she thinks.

"Mrs. Fayer," she says aloud, and the rightness of it strikes her with force. "Mrs. Eugene Henderson Fayer." She speaks the name factually, with no bitterness; it is what she has chosen for herself.

And so, at this moment, she becomes Mrs. Fayer—not Jessica Connolly, not Sister Judith, not Jessica Fayer. She has never been Jessica Fayer.

"Mrs. Fayer is standing at the window," she says. "Mrs. Fayer is waiting for the sunrise."

For a long time she contemplates her new identity, her new bleak life. She smokes another cigarette and waits.

Finally the hill and the meadow appear beyond the road; the sun is coming up.

Mrs. Fayer, exhausted before the day has begun, climbs the stairs to her room. She will dress and make the breakfasts and serve the old people.

But for how many years?

13

"And so you've got your way at last," Eugene says, whispering. His face is ashen, his full mouth has become a thin slit. "It's what you've always wanted," he says.

"What?"

"To see me like this, helpless. To have me at your mercy."

Then there is a long blank space during which she must have drunk some gin. Later he taunts her about the baby. "You've never forgiven me for it." "No, I've never forgiven you," she says. "I never will." And then she is shouting terrible things at him, her comb crushed in one hand, the palm bleeding; but she goes on, saying it all, and then much later she wakes and discovers that somehow, miraculously, Eugene has not died.

Mrs. Fayer thinks all this as she stands holding the telegram which says Eugene has died in the service of his country. The year is 1942 and Eugene is dead. She thinks back to the time before he left her as she turns the flimsy yellow paper over and over in her hands. What does this mean: to be dead? She had thought she knew all there was to know about dying.

Later a letter comes full of vague words about loyalty and dedication and Eugene's twice-tested patriotism. A government insurance check for ten thousand dollars will follow. There is nothing in the letter that says Eugene's patriotism was tested for the second time when, given the condition of his lungs and his leg, the recruiting officer shrugged and assigned him to military intelligence, foreign language division, since at least he knew Latin. There is nothing that says he was drunk when his jeep hit a high curbing and veered into a telephone pole killing him instantly. There is nothing that says he had taken the jeep without proper authorization; he had not really stolen it, only borrowed it for a trip to the local dive. The letter says nothing that could upset any newly-widowed war wife, except of course that her husband is dead. The letter is proper and imprecise and leaves Mrs. Fayer mystified.

So he is dead, Eugene Henderson Fayer.

Mrs. Fayer cries as she reads the telegram and again when the letter comes. But why should she cry? Surely, at this point, all love for him is gone. All human loves end and this one has ended time after time. His betrayals, his brutal sexuality, the lost baby, her drinking, the time she almost let him die: what love could survive all these? Or any of them? The biggest mystery, she thinks, is why he wanted to marry her in the first place. "Because I was a nun," she says aloud, answering herself, wondering if what she has said is true. "Because I was unattainable." She crumples the telegram and puts it in her apron pocket. Only half aware of what she is doing, she goes upstairs to her bedroom and takes Eugene's photograph from the top bureau drawer. She looks again at that handsome face, the heavy mouth, the jutting chin. No, he never married her for love.

She stands looking at the photograph, but she is back in the present of 1935, standing beside Dr. Turner as they listen to Eugene's labored breathing. He has pneumonia; with his weak lungs, he might easily die.

"He's in a bad way, Jess. The sulfa . . . every four hours. It could mean his life."

She has been drinking gin; she does not know why; or perhaps she does know why.

"And so you've got your way at last," Eugene says. "To have me at your mercy."

Again and again she is in this present, this awful time when she says things that can never be taken back. The comb is in her hand, her palm is bleeding. "I'm alive," she says, "and it's you who are dying." She listens to this strange voice full of hatred and revenge.

And then she is drinking again, waiting for her death.

Her mouth tastes bitter and her head throbs when she wakes in the morning. At first she cannot think where she is; this is not St. Vincent's, this is not the convent. Idly she fingers the yellow binding of the blanket and then the lace at the throat of her nightgown. If only everything could end here.

All in a rush she hears her voice of the night before; she tears back the covers and in a second she is at the door of Eugene's room. He is gray, motionless. Terrified, she moves slowly toward the bed, staring at his face, staring at his chest which does not seem to rise and fall. Lightly, trembling, she puts her fingertips to his wrist. There is a pulse.

"Oh my God, oh my God," she says, covering her face with her hands, choking with sobs. After a long while, she takes her hands away and looks at him. His eyes are open and he looks back at her. He knows.

By some miracle Eugene is still alive.

For weeks after this they do not speak. It is as if he has died after all. Eugene recovers slowly, sitting for a few hours each day on the glass sun porch wrapped in blankets, lying in bed the rest of the time. He reads the newspaper, nothing else. And he studies his wife, whom he has never known and whom he has begun to fear.

Jessica waits on him dutifully. She serves him rare roast beef and chops, though they cannot afford such luxuries, and between meals she brings him hot tea with lemon and steaming bowls of chicken broth. He has to be built up. His lungs are ruined.

They never talk. They never smile. She brings his trays of food, sets them down by his chair, and later takes them away.

What has she done in not giving him the powders, in leaving him alone to die that night? She cannot grasp it. She cannot bear to think of it. And so she waits on him, her husband, and looks after the old people and, whenever she can, she drinks.

Prohibition has been repealed for over a year now and she can buy liquor anywhere. There is no longer any need to pretend it is medicine. "Medicine," she says, pouring the liquor into a glass. "Poison is more like it." She drinks steadily throughout the day.

By the end of March Eugene has begun to take short walks when the weather is good. He goes slowly, limping, down past the barn to the lower pasture and he stands there looking into the stream. And then he comes back. Jessica watches him from the kitchen window as he comes around the corner of the barn. She is tempted to tell him the truth, that she doesn't know what happened, that she was drunk, that she did not try to kill him, to let him die, helpless and at her mercy. She is tempted, but she has a drink of gin instead.

But one day when he comes back from his walk, he does not pass through the kitchen and go up the stairs to his bed. He stops just inside the door and says in a voice that is unfamiliar to her, "Can we talk? I want to talk with you."

She is dicing onions with a huge carving knife and she does not bother to put it down. She only turns to him and says, her voice lifeless, "What is there to talk about? We have nothing to talk about."

"Come here and sit," he says. He hangs his scarf on the back of a chair and pulls the chair up to the kitchen table. She puts down the carving knife and sits opposite him. She looks straight at him, her brows arched already. She is prepared.

"Don't," he says, and drops his eyes. "I want to talk with you."

"I'm listening," she says.

"Jessica, Jessie. A lot has happened, with us, and I've been thinking about it a lot. Well, what I want to say is, I wonder if we could try . . . again."

"Again! When have *you* ever tried!"

"I know," he says. "I know. I haven't been fair, ever. Right from the start, I was to blame. I admit it. But people can change, Jessie. I can change. I *have* changed; and so have you."

She looks at him sharply, her lips pulled tight.

"Well, you have, Jessica. Ever since that night when you left me . . . and you had been warned that I could die that night . . . you've been a different person. Jessica, you're half drunk all the time."

"Liar!"

"Jessie, it's true. You know it's true." His voice is soft and pleading.

"I don't drink. You'd love it if I did. You'd have something else to lord it over me with."

"Jessica, go to the cupboard and look at the gin bottle. It was full last night. It's almost half empty now."

"Oh, so now you're a detective? Spying on me? The bottle is exactly where it was last night. You're so eager to get me in the wrong, Eugene, that you've begun imagining things. I swear to God I've never touched that bottle in the last twenty-four hours."

"Jessie."

"Well, what more do you want?"

"Jessie, I marked the bottle. I know what you've drunk."

Tears spring to her eyes. She pushes herself away from the table and goes back to the carving board where she chops the onion to small bits with the heavy knife. Eugene continues to sit at the table in silence, watching her.

"I did it for your own good," he says after a while. "I had to know how much you were drinking."

"Liar!"

"Jessie, can't we begin again? I want to try."

"I know you," she says.

"Once you loved me, Jessica. It could happen again."

She turns to him, the knife poised above the onion. "I'm not sure I ever loved you, Eugene. Perhaps I married you because I didn't want to go through life being only a nun. Perhaps it was because I wanted someone to want me." She is making these things up as she goes along. She has never thought them before, but she will remember them later. "Perhaps I needed to be needed, just as it pleased you to think somebody loved you." She turns back to the carving board and slices the onion straight down the center. She has cut it in half the wrong way, but she does not notice. "I'm not sure I have ever loved anybody."

"You did. You loved me."

"You've always thought what it pleased you to think."

He leans toward her across the table, but she will not look at him. "Jessica, don't say that. Don't say you didn't love me. You know you did." He has gone white and his voice is thin and high. "You left the convent for me. Of course you loved me."

"Is that why you married me, Eugene? Because I was a nun?" She raises her eyebrows in mock surprise. "The attraction of the unattainable? Isn't that funny. All this time I've thought it was because I was a nurse, because I could wait on the old people, because . . ."

"Don't," he says. "I'm trying . . ."

"Because I would make the perfect mother of your children."

"I said don't!"

"Children! Children! *Why* were you afraid? I've never understood *why*. Is it because I would have something of my own, something that was mine? Something besides you? Something to love . . . finally?"

They are staring at one another, silent now. Eugene's breath is coming in short gasps; a vein twitches in his forehead. The clock on the wall is ticking, ticking, and he listens to it.

"You did," he says. "You did love me."

She waits, thinking she will not say it, but then she does. "Did I?"

"Jessica!"

She puts down the knife and looks at him. "And now," she says, moving toward the cupboard, "I am going to pour myself a drink." She is calm and purposeful. She takes a tumbler and half fills it with gin. The glass is at her lips when Eugene's hand closes around her wrist, pressing hard.

"Do you know what you are?" he says. "You're a destroyer. And it's me you're trying to destroy. Me! But you don't have the courage to do it straight out—not a second time anyway—and so you're doing it to yourself instead. You're killing yourself with booze." He lets go of her wrist. "Now here. Drink it! Drink yourself to death, you destructive bitch!" He pushes the glass to her mouth, spilling the gin on her face, on her dress. His free hand moves to her throat and then falls away. He turns from her and, picking up the heavy knife, he plunges it into the carving board. "Christ," he says, and his voice is strangled.

Even after he has stormed from the kitchen, the knife continues to quiver in the board, and Jessica leans against the cupboard watching it, waiting for the blade to come to rest. She closes her eyes, willing it to stop. And then she pours herself another drink.

By the end of April Jessica's drinking has settled into a regular pattern. She is vague and only slightly drunk all during the day, but once dinner has been served and the old people are done with for the night, she drinks heavily. And on Sunday she is drunk all day, making no pretense about it. She stays in her room, sprawled only half-conscious across the bed, while Eugene cooks the dinner and serves it and cleans up afterward. She has grown blowsy looking and she does not care.

Eugene has mentioned the drinking to Dr. Turner, who gave him a cold look and said merely, "Do you wonder why?"

But later he speaks to Jessica. "I'm a doctor, Jess," he says, "and this is a medical problem. You've got to go easier on the alcohol."

"I don't drink," she says. "He'd like you to think so. But I don't. Oh, I have a tiny glass sometimes during the day because of my nerves. And at night I take it, but only to make me sleep. Living like this . . ." and she looks around her, lost.

"I know," Dr. Turner says. "I know." And leaving, he says, "Try not to worry, Jess. It can't last forever."

At the end of May, Eugene makes one last attempt.

"I'm not asking you anymore, I'm telling you, Jessica. You're destroying yourself and you're trying to destroy me. But you're not going to do it. Either we're going to start again, and try, or I'm getting out."

In her mind she is going up a dark stairwell. She is almost at the top. She wants to say "Yes, yes," but she is afraid of whatever is at the top of the stairs. She does not turn back; she only stands there, peering into the darkness, terrified.

"Do you understand, Jessica? This is an ultimatum."

The darkness is too much for her. She shrugs, and turns from him.

Eugene is driving the car again, he has recovered. He is out of the house for several hours every day. He is at the bank negotiating a new mortgage on Hillside. The times are just beginning to improve, people are working again, and soon they will have money enough to put their loved ones in a home. And so he gets his mortgage, nine thousand dollars, and the next day he is gone.

He leaves Jessica a note saying only, "You can have the house. I've taken my half. Find someone else to destroy. Try Turner—he's partial to drunks."

"He's gone, Jessie," Dr. Turner says later, though he has not seen the note.

"I did it," she says. "It's my fault."

"What I mean is, don't you think it's time to stop? You're only destroying yourself this way."

"Yes, that's what *he* said."

"Well, he was right about that anyway."

She lights a cigarette, her hand trembling.

"I'll stop for *you,*" she says.

"No, it has to be for yourself. You have to choose yourself."

"I'm not very good at making choices."

But she stops drinking that day. And now seven years have passed and it is the present, 1942, and Eugene has given his life in the service of his country. A government letter has come, very general and uninformative. And he has left Jessica his insurance money. Why?

She studies his handsome face in the photograph, but no answers are there. She dusts the frame and stands the picture on the bureau next to her jewel box. "Find someone else to destroy," she says. No, she will never get involved again. Never.

"Eugene Henderson Fayer," she says.

"Mrs. Fayer." She turns away from the picture. "Well, it was a choice I made."

14

"I don't think it's ever going to let up," Ruth Price says as she looks out the window at the rain. Rain has been falling for days and even here, in the convent guest parlor, everything seems damp.

Sister Judith ignores the remark about the weather. She leans forward in her chair and touches her friend on the knee. "Tell me," she says. "It always helps to talk about things."

"If only we could go out for a walk, I could talk outside, but the rain . . ." and she tips her head toward her daughter, Jessie, who is almost eight years old and who sits solemnly on the end of the couch listening to the two women talk. "Maybe Jessie could visit the chapel, do you think?" She gives Sister Judith an apologetic look.

There must be even worse trouble this time.

Sister Judith takes the little girl by the hand and leads her through the cloister door, down the corridor, and into the chapel. A nun is dusting around the altar, genuflecting as she crosses back and forth in front of the tabernacle. The chapel is dark and the nun's white habit seems a patch of light, moving effortlessly beneath the huge gold cross. Jessie moves closer to Sister Judith as they kneel to pray.

"What is she doing?" Jessie asks in a whisper.

"She's cleaning." Sister Judith speaks in a tone that indicates they must not talk in chapel. At once, she relents. "If you say three Hail Marys in a church you visit for the first time, you can ask God a favor and he'll grant it." Should she have said that? It's a harmless superstition. She smiles at the little girl, Jessie, who has been named after her.

Sister Judith kneels up straight, her face serene, her whole body composed in the attitude of prayer. But she is not praying. She is thinking of her friend, Ruth Price. Ruth Price Merrick Kelly, to be exact, since at age twenty-six she has been married three times and divorced twice. She married Bill Price when she was sixteen and pregnant; a year later Bill was killed fighting in a place called the Ardennes. The next two marriages ended in divorce. Her fault, she said. "I'm weak, Judith, I just like men. I like new men." And so she is back, as she has been back before each previous marriage, to ask Sister Judith what she ought to do. And always, of course, she does what she wants to do, what she has already decided to do.

Sister Judith kneels in chapel next to Jessie Price, thinking, you are the victim, poor child, you are the one to suffer. Sister Judith bends to her, slipping one arm around her shoulder. "Have you said your three Hail Marys?" she asks. The little girl does not answer, but instead throws her arms around her in a tight embrace, burying her face in the white habit. Sister Judith holds Jessie in her arms, confused, worried, and after a moment she pats the child's back and says, "Yes, yes." Jessie loosens her hold and leans away from Sister Judith. She tosses back her long dark curls, her huge gray eyes glisten, and she says, "I asked God to let me stay here with you."

Sister Judith is kissing Jessie on the forehead. What can she do? What can she say?

Jessie Price is almost eight years old and her prayers will be answered.

As Sister Judith comes back into the parlor, Ruth stubs out her cigarette against the sole of her shoe. She drops the butt into her pocketbook. "I'm sorry," she says, "I needed one."

Sister Judith sits close to her, this woman who has been married three times and who is still a child. Poor Ruth. Poor Jessie. Sister Veronica is right—all human loves come to an end.

"Tell me," she says.

"Oh Judith," and she raises her fist to her temple and then lets it fall to her lap. "It's worse this time. This time it's really bad."

"Is he married?"

"Yes!" she says. "Exactly! How did you ever know? How did you guess?"

"Ruth, dear Ruth." She takes Ruth's hands in her own, her eyes warm with affection and with hurt. "I knew it had to be a man, and I knew that if you could marry him, you would. So he must be married already."

"Oh, I see." Ruth opens her pocketbook and takes out a handkerchief which she begins to twist between her fingers. "Well, it's a little more complicated than that, you see. Judith, I . . . well, you know how weak I am, how I like men, new men. It's true, I do. I can't help it. Well, I don't know how to say this exactly, but the problem is that . . . I'm pregnant."

"Oh Ruth."

"Yes. And he's married."

The clock on the mantel ticks the minutes away. The large hand jumps and then for a long time, for years, there is a ticking sound as everything changes, as nothing changes, and then the large hand jumps again. What Sister Judith will remember about this day, the last time she will see her friend Ruth, is this moment when time is suspended and the only sound is the clock ticking on the mantel.

"I'm over five months pregnant," Ruth says, twisting her handkerchief. "And I'm afraid."

Ruth does not say why she is afraid. She does not tell Sister Judith that she has paid three hundred dollars to a doctor in South Boston, that she will pay him another three hundred, and then he will perform the abortion that will end her life. There are some things she cannot tell her friend and so Ruth says only, "I'm afraid," and rushes on.

"What I want to ask you, Judith, is for Jessie. I mean, I have no one; *she* has no one. If anything happens to me, if I die in labor or anything, will you promise to take her? I don't want her in a home, a public place. I want her with you at St. Vincent's. Promise me, only that, promise."

"Ruth, Ruth," she says, comforting a child. "Nothing is going to happen like that. You're exaggerating. You'll have the baby and . . ."

"Promise me, Judith."

"Yes, of course, of course. I promise."

Ruth dabs at her eyes with the shredded handkerchief. "Oh, the mascara," she says, and then suddenly, "I don't think it's ever going to let up, the rain."

"It will. It looks to be clearing now, in fact."

The two women stand at the window together and watch as the cold rain falls. They will stand like this forever, in a present that can never change; that is how things are for them.

"I'll get Jessie from the chapel," Sister Judith says, "and then I'll fix us all a lovely cup of tea."

But on the way to chapel she stops, remembering the doll. She should give little Jessie something, some gift, but she has nothing to give except the antique doll Sister Veronica had once—how many years ago—given to her. A china doll, dressed in white lace of the 1800s, and with a white silk parasol; it is the perfect thing for Jessie.

Sister Judith hurries to the trunk room in the basement. It is dusty, hung with cobwebs. The new Sisters' trunks are piled near the door where they can be easily reached if the Sisters decide to leave. Her own trunk, never used, had been assigned to her on the death of a very old nun who, like Sister Judith, had never used the trunk either. It stands apart from the others, unlocked, in the far corner of the room; it contains only the doll.

Carefully she removes the linen sheet and then the layers

and layers of tissue paper that encase the doll, until finally the head is exposed to the dim light. The yellow curls that line the forehead have come partly unglued and the doll's china face is crazied with a thousand blue cracks. It is ruined. Even the lace dress has turned to tatters.

"No," Sister Judith says, covering the doll's face. "Oh no." For a moment she kneels by the trunk, her eyes closed, and then she opens them and sees that the little silk parasol with the ruffles has remained somehow perfectly intact. She snatches it up and, leaving the trunk lid open, hurries off to the chapel and Jessie.

Jessie is thrilled with the parasol; she kisses it and hugs it to her chest.

"Look, Mother," she says. "Look what Sister Judith gave me," and she opens and shuts the tiny parasol.

"Yes, dear," Ruth Price says. "See how much Sister Judith loves you? You're a very lucky girl." And to Sister Judith she says, "I could really use that cup of tea."

15

Mrs. Fayer has been in the present now for sixty-six years. She is in Amherst, in the kitchen of the Hillside Rest Home, and she is waiting for the water to boil for tea. She stands with her back to the window, giving her full attention to Jessie Price.

Jessie Price, or Mrs. Price as she prefers to be called, sits at the kitchen table trying to find the right words for this situation. Usually she has no trouble finding words; words are her life. She is famous at Vassar for the clarity and intelligence of her lectures in modern philosophy and she is the author of two books, *Fear of Dying* and *Ascent to Doubt*. But here in this sprawling kitchen with Mrs. Fayer, she finds that her thoughts resist formulation in words. Why, after all, has she come?

"Perhaps after we have tea," Mrs. Price says. The problem, she thinks, is with Mrs. Fayer. Who would have thought Sister Judith could be transformed into this dull contented woman, not concerned with the life of the mind or with abstract ideas, concerned only with making a cup of tea, looking after old people? This is what can happen to a woman in our society, this living death. But is it possible for Sister Judith? Yes; the person Mrs. Price has come here to see simply does not exist. "You don't mind?" she says, lighting another cigarette.

"Of course, of course, please," Mrs. Fayer says.

Can this be Jessie Price?

Can this be Sister Judith?

Mrs. Price is a stout woman of fifty. She wears her hair short, cropped almost like a man's, and she has on a white blouse and a tweed suit. The suit is pink and gray and somehow emphasizes the whiteness of her skin and those large gray eyes, piercing, full of intelligence. She has a crease down the center of her forehead, a perpetual frown that indicates she is thinking, not that she is cross. She smokes compulsively, lighting a new cigarette from the end of the old one, squinting as she lets the smoke filter upward before her eyes. She smokes even during her lectures at Vassar, so that she seems always to be speaking from behind a veil. Her students call her The Sybil. Only the eyes convince Mrs. Fayer that this woman, polite but formidable, could possibly be Jessie Price.

And Sister Judith? Sister Judith has become Jessica, a drunk, an adulteress, a widow. Later she has become Mrs. Fayer, a woman gone heavy in her thirties, but trim once again and active. She does not look her age, partly because her hair has remained that same reddish-brown without a streak of gray, and partly because the aging process seems to have stopped in her many years back. She is a business woman; she has built a new wing on Hillside and she has more than twice the old people she had when Eugene left her. Perhaps her work is what keeps her young. Or perhaps it is Dr. Turner, who, once Eugene was reported dead, told her he loved her, he had always loved her. She had kissed him then and said no, she would never be involved again. Never. But her mind reeled: somebody had wanted her. Her! She began to dress better and fix her hair more carefully. She has kept young.

Standing with her back to the kitchen window now, she does not think of her age or of Dr. Turner, she thinks of Mrs. Price who is looking at her through the thin veil of smoke. What is it Mrs. Price can be seeing?

Mrs. Price watches Mrs. Fayer standing at the window, chewing on her lower lip. Sister Judith? No, nothing remains of Sister Judith except the eyes. Her eyes are deep green still, with gold flecks around the iris, but they are not warm any longer, they are . . . what? . . . hurt, suspicious. Only the eyes remind Mrs. Price that this woman was once her own Sister Judith.

And so they sit in the kitchen drinking tea.

"Eugene Fayer?" Mrs. Price says.

"Eugene Henderson Fayer." She smiles only slightly as she says his name.

"When did he die?"

"In the war, in '42."

"So you've been alone since 1942."

"Oh no, for much longer than that." She wants to give Mrs. Price something. She wants to recognize the Jessie Price she used to know. "He left me before that. He left me in the spring of '35."

Mrs. Price sips her tea and frowns.

"He left you. And did you think you loved him? At the time, I mean."

"Did I love him? Yes, I did. I loved him when I married him, but I don't know for how long." Should she be saying these things? Yes, to Jessie Price, but not to this stranger. But she ignores the stranger and goes on. "He never loved me, you see. He wanted me only as long as I was a nun. It was never really *me* he wanted." She shifts in her chair and looks straight at Mrs. Price. "He used to say 'I need you,' and I suppose I wanted to be needed. Or he needed to be wanted." She laughs a little: she had not meant to turn a phrase; she is not exactly sure what she has said.

"That's the basis for most marriages, I think." Mrs. Price laughs too and the frown vanishes; suddenly she is young and lovely again. Yes, she is Jessie Price.

Both of them are young once more; Jessie Price is twelve years old, she is solemn and intelligent. She walks by the side of Sister Judith who talks in that rich hypnotic voice. She listens to everything Sister says and she remembers it. She tucks her hands in her sleeves, like Sister Judith, and she practices in the bathroom mirror making her eyes soft and warm like Sister Judith's. They will never part.

"I should never have married. I'm not made for marriage. I should have stayed in the convent and been safe," Mrs. Fayer says.

"Safe? Safe from what? From the world?"

Mrs. Fayer thinks for a moment. Yes, she wonders, safe from what? How can you be safe if you're not dead?

"From myself, from what I've discovered in myself. I was happy in the convent."

"I doubt that anyone is truly happy, least of all nuns."

"Oh, that's not so. The happiest people I've ever known were nuns. Of course, they had real vocations, they were chosen. I believe that, that some people are chosen. I wasn't, but still I could have had a kind of happiness there."

"Happiness. What is happiness? Nobody is ever happy for more than a minute anyway. Work is what matters, work is the only way to any real satisfaction."

"Work."

And so they have come to the end again. Nothing has been said. Mrs. Fayer sits with her hands folded in her lap. Mrs. Price lights another cigarette.

Mrs. Price glances around her; the huge old-fashioned kitchen is immaculately clean. Compensation, she thinks; nuns never recover from the convent. But then nobody ever recovers from anything. That is why we all die. And that is why she is here. She must resurrect a dead Sister Judith.

"I destroyed the parasol the day I found out you left. The doll's parasol. I crushed it with my foot and then I threw it in the incinerator. I burned it. 'His love is a fire.' " She laughs, or partly laughs. "All human loves end, you used to say on those walks. Do you remember? I do. I remember every word you said. Even now sometimes . . . some nights . . . before I fall asleep, I'm suddenly back in that bizarre place, and we're talking together, just you and me. The whole world has fallen away, there's nothing left except a broad gravel path that we walk on, and the only sound is the sound of your voice. I never speak. I never say anything. I listen to your magic voice, caressing words, caressing me with them, as if you actually know what you are doing, and care. Mind you, not a dream. I'm not dreaming when this happens. I'm awake and it's happening to me right *then*. I listen; I remember every word you said."

Mrs. Fayer is listening to Jessie Price. Yes, she knows.

"But the only true word you spoke was that: all human loves end."

"Jessie . . ."

"It was years before I realized I was no longer in love with you. Very liberating, that."

"Jessie, what can I say to you? I must have hurt you terribly, my leaving. I suppose it's too late to say I'm sorry, but for what it's worth, dear, I am."

"Sorrow is meaningless."

But Mrs. Fayer does not hear; she is thinking of that last day they were together, of Sister Veronica saying, "Leave."

"The only merciful aspect of Sister Veronica's stroke," she says, "was that she was spared knowing I left."

"Oh, she knew. And you should be glad. The only merciful aspect of any experience is knowledge."

"But how could she know?"

"I told her."

"You?"

"It was my revenge on you for leaving me."

Mrs. Fayer drinks tea and Mrs. Price draws on her cigarette.

"But Sister Veronica couldn't understand anything; she couldn't have understood what you meant."

Mrs. Price smiles. "Oh, she made quite an improvement shortly after you left. Of course I didn't know at the time that you *had* left, they kept that from me—you were too busy, they said, you had been transferred—but in time I found out and I told Veronica. I figured out later that it was after you'd left that she began to talk again, not very much, just enough to be able to complain. She complained constantly; complains, I should say, since she's still alive."

"And you told her."

"It was a human thing to do. It was natural under the circumstances."

Mrs. Fayer says nothing. She is still thinking about Sister Veronica, who must be ninety, who has spent all these years . . . how? This is the worst betrayal: that Sister Veronica knows about her. Her face begins to crimson and her breath grows short.

"I forgive you. I forgave you on the day I realized I was no longer in love with you."

"And she's still alive!"

"I said I forgive you."

"You forgive me? For what? For leaving you? Jessie, it was the convent I left, not you."

"From your point of view, of course. That's precisely what makes perspectives so interesting. For four years you molded my psyche, my feelings, my whole being, and then one day without warning or preparation of any kind, you cut yourself off from me—from that psyche, those feelings you had molded—and you say you left religion and not me? Oh Judith, I don't think you're being honest with yourself. Or even very intelligent. No, you left me. And, as the situation eventuated, your action was very instructive, healthy even. I learned an essential lesson about life, one I had not been able to absorb so long as it remained an abstraction: all human loves end. It was just as you said. It is why I have become a lover of women."

"A lover of women?"

"Yes, I am a homosexual. Does that shock you?"

Mrs. Fayer leans away, shocked and a little frightened.

"Can you really be surprised at that, you of all people?"

"I've never known anyone who . . . like that."

Mrs. Price studies her, pleased.

"Why do you say me of all people?"

"It's evident, I should think. Because it all began with you. Life in the convent or in the convent orphanage is merely lesbianism without sex. Surely that's clear to you after all this time." She pauses for a reply, but there is none and so she continues. "And of course it all began with you, loving, learning about the fallacies of loving, the pretenses. It's ironic, I suppose, to have learned about love in a Catholic orphanage."

"Jessie . . ."

"It's ironic, too, that it wasn't until I realized that I was no longer in love with you, that I realized what my love for you had been. Oh, I don't mean sexual, though I'm sure that was there too. And I emphatically do not mean that old business of the spiritual cliché, you know, that all God's creatures are to be loved, *atqui* you are one of his creatures and pretty special too, *ergo,* you're for me. No, nothing that bald, that naive. What I realized about my love for you, Judith, was this: it was the simple human hunger for intimacy, something I have come to understand fully only in the past few years. I'm going to do a book on it, actually. It's a fascinating subject, the hunger for intimacy which is really a hunger for wholeness. People call it love." She laughs to herself quietly for a moment. "Imagine, love. Of course it is delusion: there can be no human interpenetration, either of the mind or spirit, and certainly not of flesh. Men and women only fool themselves when they think that by their grotesque couplings they have somehow united their spirits, their essential selves. Rather, they satisfy a momentary biological craving, which indeed makes perfectly good sense, so long as you don't delude yourself about the nature of the act at hand. It is precisely for that reason that I am a lover of women; because I refuse to delude myself. My encounters with women are brief and uncomplicated by intersexual emotions and demands. They're mutually satisfying. And further, they are recognized by both of us for what they are: the momentary relaxation of a neural strain."

Mrs. Price stubs out her cigarette and prepares to pounce. "But love . . ."

"All human loves end, Judith."

"Jessica. My name is Jessica, not Judith."

"Of course. It's difficult for me. All these years I've thought of you as Judith. That was your existence for me. You were never Jessica, never Mrs. Fayer."

Mrs. Fayer is in the present, in Amherst, and she is sixty-six years old. She is having tea with Jessie Price who has just said incredible things. Jessie Price, Mrs. Price, must be mad, and yet she teaches philosophy at a famous college and she writes books that people read and discuss on television. And somehow, she says, it all began at St. Vincent's on those harmless walks.

Mrs. Fayer is not here any longer; she is walking the path up the hill to the cemetery. The white gravel shines beneath her feet and the leaves of the elm tree are yellow green. She is not listening to Mrs. Price, who goes on talking about systems of logic, systems of moral values. She is listening to Sister Veronica who is young and beautiful and glides along the path, not even touching it. Sister Veronica, who is still alive and suffering.

A door slams loudly somewhere in the house and then another door slams. Mrs. Price stops talking and Mrs. Fayer comes back from her walk to the cemetery.

Martha has come in to help with dinner. Martha is young and shy. She is perhaps only fifteen or sixteen, but already she has a woman's body and a woman's walk. She works at Hillside each day when school lets out, helping prepare the dinner and then serving it. The old people like her because she is always happy and because they can tease her about her boyfriends. They watch from the sitting room window each evening to see which boy will pick her up after work. Martha's ambition in life is to get married.

Mrs. Price has decided to stay for dinner. She has driven all the way from New York for a purpose and she is not going to leave until she has accomplished it. So she sits at the kitchen table snapping beans while Martha scrubs the new potatoes and Mrs. Fayer prepares the rack of lamb. Mrs. Price is perfectly content, seeing nothing incongruous about her being in this kitchen with these two other women, so different from herself, so lost. Mrs. Price is a professor at Vassar College, she is achieving wholeness; snapping beans is only incidental to that. What does it matter that all human loves end. Wholeness is all.

Word has gone around Hillside that there will be a guest at dinner. The old people are pleased, excited. They talk to Mrs. Price about themselves, interrupting, not listening. For a minute they are important, they exist, they are not dead yet. They talk rapidly because the meal will be over soon, too soon.

Mrs. Price eats her lamb, listening, measuring her new observations against all she has said in *Fear of Dying*. Yes, she was right, she was insightful. There is nothing new here; only the old insights being corroborated. But two cases do catch her interest: old Butley from Georgia and the woman who doesn't speak. Butley could be dealt with in a footnote, she suspects; he may well be just another example of southern sexual decadence displaced by age and by life in the north. Still, he could stand looking into. The woman who doesn't speak is another matter. Mrs. Price has watched her carefully from the start of the meal and has been impressed by the quickness of her reactions. She anticipates the punchline before the joke is finished and she passes dishes before they are requested, but all that is normal in old people who have remained alert and who are hypertense. What is unusual about her is the way her mouth plays with a half-smile when something fatuous or egotistical is said. She not only listens, she judges, and she is a very discerning and demanding judge. And yet she does not speak. Mrs. Price files her away for future investigation; she might fit handily into her next book, *Wholeness and Otherness.* It will be a study in the intergration of personality: it will be her best book, her triumph. She turns again, automatically, to old Butley who is winding down now that dessert has come and the meal is over.

The old people smile at her sadly; she has been a good guest and they do not like to see her go. She may be the last guest they will ever see.

Finally it is done. The dishes are washed and wiped and put away, the old people have all gone to their rooms, Martha closes the kitchen door and leaves. Mrs. Price and Mrs. Fayer remain alone in the kitchen.

"You were wonderful with old Butley at dinner, Jessie. Thank you for doing that."

"Do you say things to her, too? Do you form her? Martha?"

Mrs. Fayer frowns and says nothing.

"Now you're hurt." She interrupts herself to light a cigarette. "I'm interested only. I imply no criticism whatsoever; the issue is purely academic, Judith. Jessica, rather. Sorry."

"No, I don't *form* her. I don't *say* things to her."

"Well, I imagine with her it would be rather difficult anyway. Her whole future is determined by the way she walks."

"I find it better not to be involved. Martha is a good girl; she's sweet and she's . . . well, happy."

"Involved! It's not *possible* to be involved, not really. It's possible only to influence."

What does that mean? What does one say to that?

During the dinner, which was relaxed, which went quickly with Mrs. Price chatting and nodding, Mrs. Fayer had forgotten the dizzying conversation of the afternoon. All the strange talk about homosexuality and systems of logic fell away in the presence of this practical bulky woman in her pink and gray tweed suit, listening to the old people as if she cared about their lives. She had not been Jessie Price, it is true, but she had not been this stranger either, this professor of philosophy obsessed with . . . with what?

"Would you like something to drink?" Mrs. Fayer asks. "I always have a drink at the end of the day."

"Bourbon, thank you." She will have to follow up on involvement later.

"I have only scotch and brandy, I'm sorry. Scotch for me, brandy for patients."

"Scotch, then. I'm adaptable."

Mrs. Fayer drinks scotch. It is good for her heart, Dr. Turner says, when he comes by each night to have a drink with her. He had done this for years, ever since Eugene's death, and he will be here this evening too. Mrs. Fayer pours the drinks and wonders what Dr. Turner will make of Mrs. Price.

"Is that all right?" she asks.

"That's fine."

"Not more ice."

"Ice is bad for the stomach. I use only a little."

They take their drinks into the front parlor and before they sit, Mrs. Fayer stands for a moment looking out the window. She is thinking, Jessie Price is a homosexual and I am to blame. She sips at her drink and then, because she must, she sits down to face this complicated woman.

"Why do you call yourself *Mrs.* Price?"

"Ah, that began long long ago, when I first began teaching. Protective coloration. If colleagues think you're divorced, they don't consider that you might be homosexual. It was necessary at the time."

"*Mrs.* It's strange, isn't it, what that word does? I think of myself as Mrs. I talk to myself—I'm getting like the old people, I suppose—when I talk to myself, I call myself Mrs. Fayer. *Mrs.* Not Jessica, but Mrs. Fayer. I thought once that it's because I've stopped being myself, that I've become some other person who married Eugene Henderson Fayer and who does the washing and cooking and who . . . oh, I don't know. It's foolish, I suppose."

"Names are incidental. No matter what you call yourself, you remain you. And I remain me. Separate."

"Yes."

"Though named after you."

"Yes. Your mother and I were close."

"I don't remember her; I remember you." Mrs. Price frowns, trying to recall her mother. No, it is useless. Her mother was no influence, not a formative influence. She was just somebody called Ruth Price, and she died.

"It was she who asked me, just before she died, to take care of you if anything happened to her." For a second Mrs. Fayer is Sister Judith again, back in that convent parlor, rain tapping at the windowpane.

"How did she die, my mother?"

"She died . . ." There is no point in telling the truth. Some truths should never be told. "She died having a baby."

"Yes, that's what they told me." In the silence that falls between them, Mrs. Fayer sips at her drink and Mrs. Price filters a cloud of smoke through her lips. "I never believed them."

"Ruth was lovely. So popular. So alive."

"But you took me in. You were the influence on me."

"I tried. I tried to be for you what Sister Veronica had been for me."

Mrs. Price laughs, a short harsh sound.

"I didn't become a . . ."

"A homosexual. A lesbian, if you like. I've always preferred the term homosexual; it emphasizes the Greek roots of the word. I am concerned with roots."

Mrs. Fayer shudders. She is cold.

"That is why I have come, Judith. Jessica. I have a theory of wholeness and otherness, which I'll try to state in its simplest form. My experience has taught me that the human drive we have for ages denominated 'love' is in fact no more than the innate motion toward wholeness, holicity, if you wish. There is that need in all of us, by reason of the fact that we are alive, that we are human; there is that need to complete the self. The mistake psychologists have made for years is to presume that that need—to complete the self—is a manifestation of movement toward the other; in short, that it is love. It is not. It is something quite, indeed diametrically, opposite. It is an inner-directed motion toward the acknowledgment and acceptance of roots. Of what has made us what we are today. Only in finding and facing our roots can we integrate the disparate and dissonant modes of the personality, of *our* personality, and eventually with effort and honesty achieve the kind of self-realization which can never be achieved through a relationship with another. In fact, wholeness is destroyed by relationship with another." She is talking rapidly, her gray eyes flashing. "The self is a fragile, precarious construction, which *we* construct. We build, you see, on living roots. The metaphor sounds mixed only to those who do not realize that roots are a given; they are fixed, petrified, even while they are living. They are the living rock because of which the present exists and upon which the future must be built."

Mrs. Price's eyes glisten and her frown deepens as she applies her theories to her own life, to her childhood at St. Vincent's, to her love for Sister Judith. She has found the key at last, she has unlocked the door.

Mrs. Fayer studies this strange woman, with the crease in her forehead, with the pink and gray tweed suit. She says she is a lover of women. She says that she—Sister Judith—is to blame.

"And what does this have to do with me? I didn't make you a homosexual."

Mrs. Price sits back in her chair, astonished. She has just explained all that.

"Again," she says. "I'll try to explain again. The homosexuality is incidental, it means nothing now. Homosexuality, hermaphrodiety, they are only states of the mind in any case. Read Jung. Look at the oldest representations of the gods. They have the organs of *both* sexes. Not because the early human was hermaphroditic, but because somehow, primitively, intuitively, she realized that in herself—or himself—were *both* sexes. We are all half men, half women. We become whole persons, not by turning outward to either man or woman—that, as I say, is incidental—we become whole by turning inward. One's sexuality does not matter. It has nothing to do with what I'm talking about."

"Then I don't know *what* you're talking about. I don't understand. You talk on and on, and you seem to be holding me responsible for something."

"But you are, you see. Exactly. You are responsible. For *me:* for that self, fragmentary and incomplete by any standard, that self you left me with when I was twelve years old. *You* made me *that*. Whether that was good or bad is a moot point. The important point is that it must be acknowledged."

"By me."

"No, no, you miss the point. By me."

"Then why do you tell me this . . . that you are a homosexual and that I have made you what you are. Is it to punish me?"

"Punish you! But don't you see? I'm trying to give you something. I'm offering you the kind of wholeness that I've discovered for myself."

"Are you, Jessie? Are you trying to give me something?"

"Yes! Yes!"

"I think you've come here out of hatred. I think you've come here out of cruelty."

"I won't listen to that. I won't let myself be sidetracked by your emotions. I'm here to give you something. You can accept what you have made me. You must, now, before it's too late."

"I don't accept it. I think we live our own lives, we make our own choices. The unhappiness we make for ourselves is our own doing. The people we choose to love . . ."

"Love! Love! You don't know what you're talking about. All love ends in death. It isn't love that matters. It isn't love!" She is desperate now. She is imploring, she is beseeching. The words tumble from her lips in perfect order, with flawless logic. The ash falls from her cigarette onto her lap, but she does not notice. She is looking over Mrs. Fayer's head, speaking to a packed lecture hall. But she has dropped the mask of scholarly objectivity. She speaks with all the passion of her life. She has the power to convert, to make her audience see the truth, to change their lives forever.

At last she comes to the end of her speech.

"Love endures only a little while," she says, "love is the last illusion." Her hand trembles as she stubs out her cigarette with finality. Her breath comes in little gasps.

Mrs. Fayer waits while the grandfather clock ticks the minutes away. Mrs. Price sips at her drink and tries to light another cigarette, but her hands shake and the lighter falls into her lap. The two women sit in silence, Mrs. Fayer waiting, Mrs. Price gripping the arms of her chair.

"Jessie, I'm old," Mrs. Fayer says at last. "I'm sixty-six years old and I'm tired. I don't understand you. I don't understand what you think it is I have done. If I've hurt you, I'm sorry. Truly I am. I never intended to hurt. I only loved you."

"You've never hurt," Mrs. Price says. "You've never meant to." And suddenly the frown in her forehead crumples and her face contorts as the tears leap to her eyes. "I know. I know." She runs a handkerchief back and forth beneath her eyes. "I had to come. I'm sorry. I had to do it. I had to let you know before it was too late." She has control of herself now, almost, and she draws herself up straight and looks accusingly at Mrs. Fayer. And then, suddenly, she collapses altogether. "Oh God, how you hurt me! Christ in heaven, you'll never know!" She grinds her fists into her stomach and bends in two as the tears pour down her face. Her whole body is shaken by the violence of her sobbing. And then, after a time that seems endless, she moans once, horribly, and is silent.

"I'll get you another drink," Mrs. Fayer says, and leaves her alone in the parlor. She is a long time in the kitchen, standing numb at the window over the sink, and when she returns she sees at once that Mrs. Price has combed her hair and put on lipstick. She is her old self. It is as if the hysterical scene had never occurred.

"Well, I must be going," she says, stubbing out the cigarette she has just lit. "Thank you," she says. Her mind elsewhere, she takes the drink from Mrs. Fayer and downs it in one long swallow. "Fine," she says, handing back the glass. "I've accomplished what I came to do; I've settled with the past. I can go now." She is speaking softly, but not to Mrs. Fayer. She is not speaking to anybody.

The two women stand together at the door, shaking hands.

Has she come to Amherst, this stranger, this Mrs. Price, has she come all the way from New York only to say unspeakable things and then leave? Why? For what conceivable purpose? For a second she is filled with scorn for Mrs. Price, and then at once a new emotion sweeps the scorn away. They have been friends, after all. Surely, once, they loved one another. Mrs. Fayer decides to risk everything.

"Are you *so* alone?" she says to Mrs. Price.

Mrs. Price looks outside into the darkness. "I have a 'friend' at the moment who lives with me. But she is only human. She'll desert me when the time comes. Or when someone new comes along. She is a former student of mine." One corner of her mouth turns up either in amusement or sorrow. "You see, we are not totally unlike."

Mrs. Price pulls out of the driveway as Dr. Turner is pulling in. He starts to back up to let her out, but she maneuvers her car up on to the lawn and eases past him, driving backward, without a moment's hesitation. She does not turn to look as her car passes within an inch of his.

Mrs. Price drives off into the evening, frowning, her large gray eyes fixed on the highway that lies ahead. There are lectures to give, a new and difficult book to write, there is life to be gotten through, somehow.

16

"For Sister Veronica?" the nurse says to the nun at the desk. "I'll take her." She is short and heavy and she wears pink-tinted glasses. "You come on with me," she says to Mrs. Fayer. "I'm going up there anyway. I love to see Sister Veronica. I mean, she's a really spiritual person with really terrific vibes."

The nurse tosses her short yellow hair as they go down the corridor to the elevator. Her fat legs rub together and the copy of *Demian* she always carries on her person bumps against her thigh. She is a nurse in this incarnation but she suspects, darkly, what she may have been earlier. "You a nun?" she asks Mrs. Fayer who is trailing behind her. When there is no answer, she says, "I just thought I'd ask. You can never tell any more, you know, the way they dress." At the elevator she falls silent, biting her nails, and squinting through her pink-tinted glasses.

It is 1970 and Mrs. Fayer has just recovered from her heart attack. She has taken advantage of the break in the hot weather to come see Sister Veronica today, the coolest day this month.

"I'm crazy about nuns," the nurse says as they ride up in the elevator. "I like all the nuns at this hospital; they're really terrific, you know what I mean? Spiritual."

"Yes," Mrs. Fayer says.

"I'm very into Zen," the nurse says. "I've got some thoughts."

"I'm afraid I don't know about Zen."

"Zen is the whole thing, believe me. It's the answer." She looks off for a moment to a heaven far beyond the surging elevator; she is lost in that heaven; she disappears. "I've always been like that," she says in a hushed voice, "a spirituality freak. No kidding. I mean, like, I'm not as spiritual, say, as Sister Veronica or anything, because I've got a boyfriend and all, if you get me. But I think if you're going to be really happy, you've got to be really spiritual. Zen," she says, and taking out her book, she holds it up for Mrs. Fayer to see. "*Demian*. I keep it on my person."

She walks Mrs. Fayer down the corridor and points to a room on the right. "Here we are," she says, and as an afterthought, "You know about the penicillin reaction, right?"

"You mean she's had one?"

"Oh geez, I'm sorry. I mean I really am. They should've told you or something. You see what happened is this. She had this really bad pneumonia, I mean like she wasn't gonna pull through, so they gave her a lot of penicillin. I mean, they always do, like it's the best thing. But she's so old and everything, there wasn't any record on her or anything, and, like the doctor just didn't know, so she had this reaction. I mean, it's really bad."

"Thank you for telling me." Mrs. Fayer knows what this means.

"Oh sure," the nurse says, bright again. She precedes Mrs. Fayer into the darkened room. The blinds have been drawn and Mrs. Fayer makes her way to the bed slowly, but the nurse knows her way in the dark. "There she is," the nurse says. "Isn't she an angel? I mean don't you just feel it?" She smiles at Sister Veronica and then at Mrs. Fayer. "Well, see you," she says and bustles from the room, *Demian* smoldering against her thigh.

Mrs. Fayer has not looked at the figure in the bed. She is trying to prepare herself for what she will see there. "My

Jesus, mercy," she says, and is surprised, because she has not prayed in years.

Sister Veronica lies in bed with her eyes open, her chest rising and falling as she breathes. There is a small white veil over her hair, and she wears a short nightgown. Otherwise her body is totally exposed to the air. Her legs are kept parted so that they will not touch; her arms have been placed away from her body. She is covered with blisters. Some have begun to form scabs, but mostly she is raw patches of burned flesh. Her face is very small and very dark and her eyes have sunk deep into her head. The smell of dying fills the room.

Mrs. Fayer approaches the side of the bed carefully and stands there, praying. She wants to touch the dying woman, to kiss her, but where? She fights back the tears.

For a half hour she stands by the bed, but then the pain around her heart begins and she knows she must leave. There are worse things than death, she thinks, and she is filled with an enormous desire to live, to love somebody. It was cowardly not to risk everything with Dr. Turner. To love him. To let herself be loved. She bends close to the pillow, whispering into Sister Veronica's ear.

"I love you," she says. What else could mean anything now?

Sister Veronica's lips move, but no sound comes out. Mrs. Fayer turns to go, when suddenly she hears Sister Veronica's voice, distorted, broken.

"I can't die," she says.

Mrs. Fayer stands there, helpless, watching two small tears tremble in Sister Veronica's eyes.

"I can't die," she says again.

Mrs. Fayer leaves then, but on the elevator she meets the yellow-haired nurse with *Demian,* who nudges her in the ribs and says, "Really spiritual. I mean *really,* right?"

17

Mrs. Fayer sits back, surprised to discover she is happy, that she has been happy for many years now. She has been reading a book by Edith Wharton and she has come to a passage that says: "There are lots of ways of being miserable, but there's only one way of being comfortable, and that is to stop running around after happiness." Yes, that's right, that's true. She has stopped running around after happiness and she finds it has come to her anyhow. Perhaps that's the way everything is.

She glances at the clock; 8:30; Dr. Turner won't be here for another half hour. She gets up and heats a cup of milk. She will have cocoa while she waits for him. She looks around the kitchen, which is spotless, and she thinks, yes, she has been lucky after all. She has been able to work. And happiness, whatever that is, has come to her without any effort on her part. And love too, or love of a sort.

She and Dr. Turner have had their hard times—after Louise's suicide attempt they did not see each other for a full year—but, given the limitations on both sides, things have turned out well. They see each other often, they laugh together, and sometimes they make love. She is fifty-two and he is fifty-six; they could be any married couple, except that he is already married. Except that words have been spoken between them that can never be spoken again.

Eugene had warned her; "you're a destroyer," he said,

and she had determined she would never be involved again. And so when Dr. Turner kissed her and said he loved her, she had shaken her head no, no it was too late, no she could never love anyone again, no she would not let herself. A year passed and they saw each other often, harmlessly, in the long evenings when the old people had gone to bed and the house was silent and cold. And then one night, Dr. Turner said to her, "He's been dead for over a year now. Let me, Jessie. We're in our forties. We're not children. Before it's too late, let me." And she took him to bed for the first time. They made love, she silent and breathless, he telling her he loved her, only her. In the morning, in the time just before dawn, he got up and went home. Not every night, but often, they lay together for hours while she clung to him and listened for Eugene's curse, and he said, "I love you, Jessie. Oh God, I love you." The day came, finally, when she said it. She couldn't help herself, she thought, she couldn't keep it back any longer. "I love you too," she said, "but oh, Henry, I'm afraid, I'm afraid." It was what he had been waiting for. He told his wife, Louise, that he wanted a divorce, that there was another woman, that he and she were done. And the next night while Dr. Turner and Mrs. Fayer planned a new life together, Louise Turner took the pills she had saved and, getting into a tub of hot water, slit her wrists, a little, enough to let them know what she could do if they forced her to it. Dr. Turner and Mrs. Fayer did not see each other for a full year after that.

Mrs. Fayer stirs her cocoa, blowing on it. It is still too hot. But time changes everything, she thinks, and she goes back to her book and reads the passage again. "There are lots of ways of being miserable, but there's only one way of being comfortable, and that is to stop running around after happiness." Yes, yes.

There is a tapping at the kitchen door, which opens at once, and it is Dr. Turner, smiling because he is early. His shock of blond hair has gone white over the years, and his lean frame is heavy, but he is handsome still, and he is in love.

"Ah," she says, "it's happiness himself. You're early tonight." She moves easily into his arms.

"Christ, I love you," he says, shaking his head as if he himself cannot believe it. And then he whispers, his tongue in her ear, "I love you."

She will not risk losing him another time. Never again. "I'll get you a drink," she says.

And so it is an hour later. It is two hours later. They have made love and she listens while Dr. Turner lets himself out and then she rolls on to her back and stares at the ceiling.

"I am somebody's mistress," she says aloud. "I am a fallen woman." She laughs to herself at the idea. She rolls over on her side and clutches a pillow fiercely to her, wrapping her legs around it, burrowing in it with her head. "I love you, I love you, I love you," she says, pouring out the words she must never again let him hear. She is crying now. "I love you."

"I am so happy," she says.

• • •

Jessie Price, or Mrs. Price as she prefers to be called, has just driven off after her visit and Mrs. Fayer is eager to tell Dr. Turner about it, but he is preoccupied, he is not listening.

"That's nice," he says. "It's good that you had a nice visit with her."

They are sitting at the kitchen table having their evening drink.

"What is it?" she asks.

"What is what?"

"Henry." Her tone is intimate but firm, somehow. It is the tone of people who are married and who have weathered bad years.

"Well, it's Louise," he says. "She's getting worse. She's getting really crazy."

"I thought we had agreed not to talk . . ."

"Well, you asked," he says. "You wanted to know. So know."

"I'm sorry." She uses that tone again, but he doesn't seem to notice.

"She's getting impossible. She's turning into a child. A malicious child. She calls herself Lulu. She carries around a pocketbook full of little bits of paper covered with conversations. Imaginary conversations."

"Yes?"

"*Your* conversations."

Again there is a silence between them.

"She found out who I am?"

"No. No, of course not. Or if she has, she's never let on. She thinks it's all over now, anyway. She thinks it all ended when she tried to commit suicide." He toys with his glass, he is getting angry. "She hates me. 'Look what you've done to me,' she says, and she shoves those papers at me, those crazy conversations. She thinks she's talked to you. She thinks you're after her money."

"I'm sorry."

"What's there to be sorry about?" He swallows the remainder of his drink. "Except our lives. Except *her* life."

Mrs. Fayer looks straight ahead and says nothing. He is seventy; he has a right to his anger.

"We've made a mess of it, Jessie. We've bungled it."

"We did what we thought was best."

"Best." He shakes his head and smiles bitterly.

"Another drink?"

"Why not? Why the hell not? Oh the guilt, Jessie, the goddamned guilt."

"Isn't there something you can do for her?"

"Commit her, I guess." And then he looks up at her suddenly as she stands by the sink, putting water in his scotch.

"*We* could have had something, Jess. You and me. At least somebody would have been happy."

"Would have been?"

"Yes. Once. I loved you enough, then."

Mrs. Fayer stares out the window into the dark. Once? Then? She brings him the fresh drink.

"Oh, what does it matter?" he says. "We're all done for anyway. We're old. We're dying. I'm seventy. You're what? Sixty-six? Louise is seventy-two. Why couldn't we just die and have it over with? 'This long disease, my life.' Who said that?"

"We've had something," she says. "We've been happy."

"Have we?" he says. "All I seem to remember is the guilt. I managed to make two women miserable instead of one of you happy."

"I have been happy. You've made me . . ."

"Oh Christ!" he says. "Wouldn't you once, just once in your life, wouldn't you like to break out of this, this *trap,* this belonging to other people, and just live, live, once, for yourself!"

She hears his words, but she does not listen to them. I love you, she is thinking, I love only you.

"I'm bad for you tonight, Jessie," he says. He is leaving. He is getting out. She knows it. "I'll be back, I don't know when. Tomorrow, the next day." And he goes.

Mrs. Fayer sits at the kitchen table, her hands knotted in her lap.

Jessie Price, she is thinking.

And now Henry.

What is this lump of coal that passes for a heart that she can give to no one.

"And so you've got your way at last," she says, not knowing what she means.

• • •

Mrs. Fayer is standing on the front porch chatting with the old people. It is a beautiful summer afternoon in 1969 and they are all taking the sun, rocking back and forth in the green wicker chairs.

"Ain't much of a worker, is he?" Butley says, pointing to Adam, the new handyman. Adam is sitting at the far end of the lawn, poking at the sole of his foot, while the power mower whirrs idly at a little distance. "You'd think the noise would bother him." Butley shoots her a mean little smile. "Well, you can't expect the best work from relatives, I guess."

So he's found that out too. How does he do it, she wonders.

Adam is a distant relative of Dr. Turner, a Brockway, and Mrs. Fayer has taken him in as a favor. There are drugs in his background, she knows, and some kind of literary fling in the Village or maybe in San Francisco. But he is quiet and harmless and he does the heavier work for her, though not very well. He has been working at Hillside since the beginning of summer.

"Oh, Adam is all right," she says. "Adam is . . ."

"Well, he's back!" Butley interrupts her; he is no longer interested in Adam because he has spotted Dr. Turner's station wagon at the bottom of the hill. "I thought he was gone for good." He is studying her expression but it reveals nothing.

The station wagon stops in the driveway and Mrs. Fayer walks slowly across the lawn toward it, paying no attention to old Butley. "Tell him I want to see him," he calls after her. "Tell him I have to talk to him about my stools."

"Isn't this a marvelous day," she says, keeping her distance from him, because she knows everyone on the porch is watching.

"Let's go to the kitchen, Jess. I have to talk to you."

"I have no luck with flowers," she says, just to say something. "Look at that bed of phlox there; did you ever see anything so scraggly? I wonder if they need more water. I must remember to ask Adam about that, or somebody."

Dr. Turner says nothing; he lets her go on talking until they are inside the house.

"What's wong?" she says at once. She does not kiss him, even though she has not seen him for a week.

"It's Louise," he says. "I've had her committed. To Lockwood. I can't manage her any more. She's crazy."

"Oh no."

"I had to. She's out and out crazy." He puts his hand over his eyes for a moment, as if he is shading them from the light.

"Do you want some coffee?" she says. "Can I do *some*thing for you?"

"Coffee," he says. "No, Sanka."

They sit at the kitchen table where they have sat so often, before making love, after making love, but this time they sit in silence. The kettle begins to whistle, finally, and Mrs. Fayer gets up and prepares the Sanka. Again they sit in silence. She wants to reach out to him, she wants to touch him, but he has shut himself against her somehow. It will have to be he who makes the first gesture.

"One way to look at it, I suppose," and then he pauses, as if he is deciding whether or not to say it.

"Yes?"

"One way to look at it is that we did it to her. We're to blame." He looks at Mrs. Fayer but her eyes are lowered. "The more sensible way is to presume it would have happened anyway. I guess."

"Don't say we did it. Don't say that."

"Well, didn't we?"

"I loved you, Henry. You loved me."

"Was it love? I guess it was. Anyway, whatever it was, we've been convenient for one another."

He cannot be saying this. He cannot mean this.

"Convenient! I'd give my life for you, you know that."

"Oh, life," he says. "That. Of course." He looks at her coldly, from a long distance in his mind. "Do you know that not once in the past twenty-some years have you said you love me. Do you realize that?" He is not angry; he is merely stating an odd fact.

"I couldn't. I was afraid. Oh, I wanted to, you'll never know how much. But there was Louise . . ."

"Don't," he says, and puts his hand up to stop her. "No more." He sighs, long and painfully. "I just want peace," he says. "I just want to have done with it." He gets up, an old man, exhausted, and walks slowly toward the door. "I'm sorry," he says. His hand is on the doorknob.

Done with it, she thinks. Done.

"I'll see you tomorrow, Jess."

She says nothing.

"All right?"

"Of course."

She smiles at him and her eyes are cold. She knows he will not see her tomorrow and so does he. This is the end for them. She has had her chance and she has let it, somehow, slip away from her.

"Of course," she says, watching through the window as he walks to the station wagon. "Of course."

And, without thinking that it is still a bright summer afternoon, she turns the lock on the door.

18

The year is 1970 and the mild July morning in Amherst has become a scorching afternoon in Boston. Mrs. Fayer has arrived at the bus terminal, desperate to begin a new life. Dr. Turner was right. Wouldn't you just once like to break out of this trap, he had said, this belonging to other people. Well, she would do it. She would start over.

It is thirty-five years since that morning when she began to think of herself as Mrs. Fayer. She has lived twice that thirty-five years, and she has been loved. Despite how it ended, she is sure that Dr. Turner loved her. It is she who failed him. Out of what? Out of fear, out of something. But now that is all past. She will begin a new life or die in the attempt.

On the bus she has met a crazy woman called Lulu Mercer. Could she have imagined her? She cannot be Louise Turner. No, Louise is in a mental home with all her scraps of paper. And before that, she has had a quarrel with Adam Brockway. And before that she has seen Adam and Martha wrestling at the head of the stairs that lead to Virgil's room above the garage. Oh yes, and Mrs. Price.

Mrs. Fayer goes over all these things, telling herself about Lulu Mercer and Adam and Martha, because she thinks she is dying and talking somehow delays it. But she is not dying; she is merely having a heart attack.

Mrs. Fayer is getting out of her seat. She is standing in the aisle. A young man with long hair is helping her lift her gray suitcase down from the luggage rack. It is not heavy, but he wants to help. He is smiling at her as if he knows she is frightened. He could be her child, her son, but no, her son would be forty now. She thanks him and gets off the bus. She remembers these things.

There are people at the exit gate, crowding in close to greet the passengers. No one is there to greet her and she is glad of that. Bus terminals are terrible places, filthy, full of old chewing gum and cigarette butts and spit. Derelicts are all over the place; one of them is staring at her. He is clutching a brown paper bag with a bottle inside. He will ask her for money. She walks with purpose through the long waiting room and out into the street.

Outside, steam rises from the tarred pavement. It is a sweltering afternoon. Mrs. Fayer rests her suitcase on the sidewalk for a minute and gasps for a breath of clean air. There is only tar and cement everywhere she looks.

At once a drunk pushes himself from the shade of the bus stop awning and tugs at her elbow. "Spare change," he says half-heartedly. His face is red and swollen, pus drips from one eye. Mrs. Fayer looks around her; everyone must be staring. No one is staring. She digs into her purse and finds a quarter which he looks at for a moment and then puts into his pocket as he lurches away. The fingertips of her white gloves are soiled from the palm of his hand.

Mrs. Fayer picks up her suitcase and looks back and forth. She is hoping for a taxi, but of course there is none. She must walk, even though it is too hot, even though the pain beneath her ribs is constant now. She thinks of turning back and realizes she cannot. She goes ahead.

She cuts directly across the intersection, passing in front of the Playboy Club and the Avis Car Rental, where already at three in the afternoon bloated young men with pink faces are passing from one door to the other. On her left is the Hotel Statler Hilton. On her right is the Teddy Bear Lounge, its windows full of photographs of Ineeda Mann, grinning, displaying her white siliconed breasts.

Mrs. Fayer lowers her head and walks more rapidly. It is

so hot. For a moment the cement beneath her feet wavers and comes toward her, but then it steadies, rolling out flat again before her, and she goes on. She is desperate to get to her new apartment. She knows what is happening to her and she does not want it to happen here on the street. A right at the corner, two long blocks, a left, and home. She is almost at the corner.

A girl rushes out of the lunchroom. In denim overalls and a dark blue sailor's jacket, she is dressed for winter even though it is a sweltering day in July. She is fat, with a spotty face and short black hair.

The girl approaches the woman with the suitcase, not caring that this is Mrs. Fayer whom she has never seen before, not caring that Mrs. Fayer will fall to the sidewalk with a heart attack. This girl has her own cares which Mrs. Fayer knows nothing about.

The girl stands in front of her, barring her way. The girl is staring, her milky eyes hard with hatred. She says nothing. Slowly she takes her right hand from her pocket and aims her finger, as if it were a gun, straight at the woman's forehead. She makes the noise of a gun going off, then again and again. Suddenly she screams, a high piercing wail, and runs away toward the bus station.

Mrs. Fayer continues walking. She rounds the corner, holding her chin high. She is on Arlington Street when her knees buckle and she sinks to the sidewalk.

Several people cross the street away from her so as not to be involved, but in a minute a small crowd gathers anyway.

"She's drunk, I can tell. She's drunk all right."

"No. Look at her dress, she couldn't be drunk."

The two drunks have been walking behind her all the way from the Teddy Bear Lounge. They have seen the girl come out of the lunchroom and approach the woman with the suitcase. They have seen her aim her finger, as if it were a gun, straight at the woman's forehead. They have heard her scream and they watched her as she ran away toward the bus station. But that was ages ago in some forgotten past. This is the present, they are on Arlington Street, and when they see the woman collapse on the sidewalk, they presume she must be drunk. As they argue, the crowd gathers.

"Hey, lady, are you all right?" A man with a briefcase enters the circle of bystanders and calls to the woman who is lying on the sidewalk. "Lady? Can you hear me?"

"She can't hear you, she's drunk."

"She's not drunk. How could she be drunk?"

The crowd looks from the woman on the sidewalk to the two men and then back again. They are waiting for something to happen. The sky above is blue and hard and cloudless. It is midafternoon in the center of the city, and somehow there is no sound.

A pregnant woman begins to fan herself, impatient. She sets her shopping bag on the sidewalk between her feet. "Hot," she says to no one. She leans heavily on one hip so that for a moment everyone stares at her stomach.

At last a policeman approaches and the man with the briefcase moves away from the body. "This woman, she's just lying there," he says to the policeman. He looks around and then slips into the crowd. He has disappeared.

"Okay, everybody, clear back, move away now. Give the woman some room to breathe."

No one moves. He is black and telling them to move. They shuffle their feet from side to side a little and that seems to satisfy the policeman, who kneels next to the woman.

She has not vomited. There is no sign of external bleeding. Good. Or maybe not so good. He goes to the corner police phone and calls for an ambulance. Returning, he kneels down beside her again.

The crowd has made way for him, but closes around once more. What will he do? Surely he will have to do something. They are standing on the street corner on the hottest day so far this summer. Maybe she will die. Maybe she will get up and walk away, cursing.

"God," the pregnant woman says, fanning herself.

"I know," someone answers.

The policeman tips Mrs. Fayer's head to the side so that she faces him. At once her eyes flicker, and then her whole body trembles as she twists toward him and whispers something. Her eyes are open and she is staring at him as if she recognizes him. They look at one another for a full minute and then again she says something. It sounds to him like "Virgil." What can this mean? He bends closer to her now, his black cheek pressed against her bloodless white one, and he hears her say, distinctly, unmistakably, "Enter me."

He does not look up. He does not look away from her to somebody else who will smile and nod. No one else could have heard her anyway. He only holds her, closely, carefully, for a little while.

Later, by the time they get her to the hospital, whatever foolish things she has said won't matter anyway. She is done for; he knows that look. And so he kneels, holding her in his arms.

He has work to do and he does it.

Mrs. Fayer is in the hospital and she is not done for. She is not conscious, but she is not unconscious either. She is alive and in the present.

"You'd better give her a shot," a voice says. "Fifteen mgs of morphine."

"Right away," another voice says.

So she must be in the hospital. Yes, she feels the needle probing for the deltoid muscle; they have it at last; and now slowly, softly, the pain is transformed into something else, some intense feeling, but what is it?

She is in love, she is loved. She is Sister Judith, and she is thirty years old. Her skirts rustle in a way she has never noticed before. Is it the blue apron she wears that makes that rustling sound? She is on her way to chapel to pray for guidance, though she has already decided to marry him. Eugene Henderson Fayer. Eugene Henderson Fayer.

But then the morphine takes effect and she is no longer in this present. She is not in any present. She is suspended in her pain without really feeling it. Later, a long while later, she is Mrs. Fayer again.

"There's no time like the present. You just give yourself right in to taking it easy and you're going to be fine. Just fine."

Someone is bending over her, talking. So she is alive after all; death has stopped somewhere at the foot of the bed.

"I always say there's a time for everything, and when you're flat on your back in the hospital, I say it's time for a rest. So you do it! You just keep on resting!"

The noise goes on and on. She cannot stop it. She opens her eyes.

"Mrs. Fayer? You see? There we are. You remember me, Mrs. Fayer. Lulu Mercer, that's who."

The absurd woman is bending over the bed, talking. Little curls dangle across her forehead, shaking from side to side as she talks.

"It's just me, Lulu Mercer. But, Mrs. Fayer! Mrs. Fayer? I've brought some friends. Lookee here!"

Lulu Mercer pulls someone forward, another woman, much younger. Her head is bent to the side, so that the huge gray eyes are visible only in profile. She is leaning in toward Lulu Mercer. They are in collusion. They are plotting.

"It's Jessie Price, that's who!" Lulu Mercer beams at her, showing her long yellow teeth.

Mrs. Fayer is lying in bed, saying nothing. This is all madness. She is imagining it. Something has happened to her brain and she will be like Sister Veronica. She closes her eyes and turns away from the women at the foot of her bed.

"You see! You're feeling better already."

Lulu Mercer and Mrs. Price whisper, talking behind their hands. Mrs. Fayer cannot hear what they are saying. She catches only words. My Henry, she hears, and then something about dying, about death.

With her eyes closed, it is quieter in the room. And now she hears other sounds besides the whispering. A man's voice. He has said something and now he is clearing his throat.

She opens her eyes a tiny slit. Yes, it is a man. Adam Brockway stands at the foot of the bed where the two women had been; they have moved over by the window to make room for him. Adam has someone with him, Martha, yes, it must be Martha who stands beside him with her arm around his shoulder. Martha smiles up at him, trying to catch his eye, but he does not pay any attention to her. Martha moves in closer to him and begins to trace tiny circles on his chest.

"No," he says, pushing her hand away. "I've got to see this. I've never seen anybody die before."

His eyes are fixed on the woman in the bed.

Mrs. Fayer is having trouble breathing. Her hands flutter at her sides and her chest rises and falls rapidly as she gasps for breath.

"Wait," Adam says to Martha. "Wait." But she does not wait. Her hand caresses his cheek and slips down to his neck and then to his chest.

Mrs. Fayer is choking for breath.

"Now," he says, and takes her hand and moves it lower, lower, until it disappears below his waist.

And then, suddenly, there is a respite; Mrs. Fayer can breathe again. She opens her eyes to Adam and Martha. They are cut off at the waist by the bottom of the bed, but she knows what they are doing. They grin at her, their bodies melting toegther. The two women have stopped whispering and only stare, waiting for something.

Yes, she has lost her mind. None of this can be happening.

"But you haven't," Lulu Mercer says. "That would be the easy way out. This is all to be expected. This is normal and natural. Natural and normal. You'll see. Don't you worry about that."

Mrs. Fayer closes her eyes. Everything disappears and then

reappears, changed. Lulu Mercer is no longer Lulu Mercer; she is someone else, someone familiar, but who? Nothing is what it seems to be.

"I've brought you this plant, Mrs. Fayer now, and I just want you to have it. A delphinium. I know you've got a real green thumb and there's nothing like a delphinium in the city. That's something I always say. I'll put it right on this little table by the window where it can bloom its heart out."

The voice recedes and the pain recedes with it. There is someone new standing at the foot of the bed. Touching her feet. Her feet and hands have grown cold and the cold spreads slowly up to her knees, to her elbows. Someone is touching her, an icy touch, from inside her bones, the bones in her arms and legs, and the cold touch spreads, slowly, to her groin, to her shoulders. She is being filled with this coldness. It has come from every extremity and is gathered at her heart. It is inside her, and outside too. She feels the cold prying at her heart, tentative icy fingers, exploring, probing. In a matter of seconds the hand will close and it will be over.

So this is death. It is not so terrible after all.

She is moving deeper into deep water. She is submerged in this pleasant water, drifting, floating. Sister Veronica is here, floating in this water, and Eugene, and Virgil, and Henry. She smiles. They are all transformed by the motion of the water, their faces merge and blend. Nothing is what it seems. She must be transformed herself.

And then she is rising in the water, drifting upward past the changing faces, coming slowly to the surface. There is a cool breeze across the water. She takes deep breaths of the clean bright air as she lies quietly on the water's surface. She could be happy like this forever.

When she opens her eyes, there is no one in the room. The two women are gone. Adam and Martha are gone.

It was all a dream, an hallucination. The morphine they have given her. The heart attack.

She hears her own voice saying, "I could live now." She must be imagining that too. It must be the morphine. There are any number of explanations.

But she can think of no explanation for the delphinium that stands on the little table by the window, its blooms already beginning to fade.

19

Six years ago, in 1970, Mrs. Fayer had a heart attack but she survived it and now she is living. She is having lunch at the Top Of The Hub with her friend Gordon Sloane. They lean across the heavy white linen, talking eagerly, intent.

Gordon is complaining about his marriage; it was a mistake, he tells her, he should never have done it. He is afraid of what will happen; he is afraid he will go back to the river and cruise. He's bound to do it eventually.

"Cured," he says bitterly. "Some joke."

Mrs. Fayer doesn't say anything. She only touches his hand lightly and smiles. He looks at her in a special way. Anyone seeing them would think they were lovers.

"There's your daughter," she says. "There's Jessica."

"Yes, thank God." He stares into his coffee cup. "But even she . . . I wonder, Jessie, what happened to me to make me the way I am, and I wonder if I'm doing it to her, and not even knowing. You know? We get warped by someone and then we warp the next in line. It goes from my mother to my daughter, straight through me, as if it were genetic. Or a curse."

"It?"

"You know. What I *am*. Or something else, something even worse, if there is anything worse. We say some aimless thing to a child, something we don't even think about, and it takes roots and it changes their life forever. Or determines it. Makes them happy or miserable, and we don't even know."

"It's a mystery."

Mrs. Fayer is thinking of Sister Veronica. She is thinking of Jessie Price.

"Mystery; where our lunches always end. Well thank God I have you," he says, taking her hand and squeezing it tight.

"We're the lucky ones," she says. "We've survived."

There is a small commotion at the reception desk. An old woman is quarreling with the headwaiter. She raises her voice and people turn to look. She has a row of tiny curls across her forehead and they bob back and forth as she jabs the waiter with one finger and then points at the woman accompanying her, a bulky woman, younger, who carries a white parasol with a ruffle. Mrs. Fayer knows that voice. It is Lulu Mercer and the woman with her—but it cannot be—is Mrs. Price. And then they are gone, ushered away to the elevator by the headwaiter, his arm gently but firmly on Lulu Mercer's shoulder.

"A crank," Gordon says. "The city's full of them."

"She looked familiar," Mrs. Fayer says. She has a vague idea of following the two women. But that's silly, she knows, and yet? "We ought to go," she says. "You should be at the hospital."

In the street Gordon kisses her goodbye and Mrs. Fayer walks slowly home, window-shopping along the way, all thoughts of Lulu Mercer and Mrs. Price gone completely from her head.

Mrs. Fayer is in the present and life is good. She is seventy-six years old, but she does not look it and she does not feel it. She dresses expensively from the shops along Newbury Street. She eats less and she exercises more, exploring the gardens and the narrow winding streets of Beacon Hill and the Back Bay. She has a group of friends, old people like herself, who sit every afternoon on the green benches along the Commonwealth Avenue mall. They gossip and complain and sometimes they laugh. Her friends depend upon her because she is the only one of them who is always happy.

But she has had an easy life, they think; she does not know what it means to suffer. After all, she has money and can afford to shop at expensive stores. She could travel if she wanted to. She has her health. But most important of all, she has someone who loves her. She is loved. She has Gordon and his wife and their daughter, Jessica Curtis Sloane. She carries pictures of the child in her wallet and she shows them to her friends—my godchild, Jessica Sloane. Little wonder Mrs. Fayer is always happy; what could she ever have known about suffering?

Mrs. Fayer knows they think this and, in her heart, she agrees with them. She came to Boston six years ago, angry and dying, and now she is young and has everything to live for. Gordon, little Jessica, the exciting present: everything. And all because of the heart attack. Even now she sometimes feels herself floating in the pleasant water, all the faces of her life smiling, transformed. She has died and she is alive again. Everything is possible because nothing is what it seems.

She is at Dartmouth Street, crossing over to the Commonwealth mall, when a panhandler steps out of the church portico and follows her. She puts her right hand on her pocketbook which hangs from her left wrist, not to protect it, but to give him something. She gives quarters to every one of these men who ask her, and there are many.

"I beg your pardon, Madam," he says in a deep rich voice.

"Wait till we're across," she says. "I don't want to get us both killed."

Safe on the sidewalk, he bends toward her, not exactly bowing, but making some kind of deferential gesture. He is middle-aged, handsome in a scruffy way, and though his face is solemn, he seems to be about to laugh.

"Again," he says, "I beg your pardon, Madam, but I wonder if you could spare me . . ." and she is opening her pocketbook, looking for her change purse . . . "a thousand dollars." She looks up at him, sharply. "Cash," he says.

She laughs then, a full deep laugh, and he joins her. She

looks at him closely. His face is raddled by years of alcohol; he is still a young man, but the veins stand out on his forehead and there are deep slashes of brown beneath his eyes. And yet he seems happy.

"Why, that's marvelous!" she says. "What a marvelous thing to ask anybody."

"Life is tough," he says, dropping his cavalier tone. He is confiding in her; he is talking to her as a friend. "I don't mean for me, I don't care much one way or the other, but it's rough for most people, and I figure if you're gonna ask them for money, you might as well brighten their day a little bit. A little laugh," he says, "a little joke. No harm done."

His eyes are sparkling. Is it drugs, or is it just that he is very much alive? She cannot tell.

"Do you want to buy lunch, is that it?" she says, wishing immediately that she hadn't said it.

"Well, to tell you the truth, no. What I want is a drink; no point lying, is there."

"I didn't mean . . . I know . . . I used to . . ." And then she shakes her head; it is too late; it is hopeless now. "Good," she says, and presses a dollar into his hand. She lets her fingers rest against his palm for a second, for less than a second. She wants to touch him, but she only smiles and says, "Things aren't what they seem."

"How's that?"

He folds the dollar methodically, unembarrassed, and then slips it into his pocket. He has the air of completing a business transaction.

"It's just something that came to me. Nothing is what it seems to be."

"Oh yes, I know." If he understands what she is saying, he gives no sign of it. "Well, thank you, and have a good day." He makes that gesture again, a sort of inclination of his head that is half way to a bow. He could be a priest at the altar.

"And you too," she says.

They turn in opposite directions, but after a few steps she stops and looks back at him. Abruptly he turns, surprise on his face.

"No," he says. "Nothing is what it *is*."

And he goes down the center of the mall, loping in the September sunlight.

Mrs. Fayer stands watching the figure retreat. The sunlight through the trees plays tricks on her eyes and for a moment as he bounces along the cement walk, he seems to spread his arms like some huge bird, and in her mind she sees him leaving the ground, wavering for a moment, and then lifting off, flying above the benches along the mall, above the trees, soaring like some huge ridiculous eagle above the sweltering city. And then she blinks hard, and he is walking along, normal, in a patch of sunlight at the crosswalk. He starts across the street just as a large green Mercedes bears down on him, but in three long bounds he is safe on the sidewalk, grinning.

Yes, he is alive. She watches him disappear from sight, loping still as he rounds a corner.

"Nothing is what it seems," she says, and then adds, "nothing is what it *is*." She smiles to herself, grateful to be alive, grateful to be in love, and she continues her slow walk home.

But on Marlborough Street, just as she is about to turn into her apartment, she sees two women at the end of the block. One of them is very old, with gray curls, and the other carries a white parasol. Yes, it is them. But it cannot be them.

Mrs. Fayer's pulse quickens and there is a pain beneath her ribs. She ought to go upstairs and lie down. She wonders, will they turn at the corner and see her? But they do not turn, and she is pleased; she does not want to be seen. And yes, she does want to be seen.

But who are these women? What are they to her?

She hears Gordon saying, "It goes from my mother to my

daughter, straight through me, as if it were genetic. Or a curse," and for a second she makes some connection between these women and what he has said. But instantly it is gone.

Mrs. Fayer decides to follow them just to the Public Garden. She pauses in the shade of a giant elm, where it is blessedly cool. She leans against the tree and watches the two women who continue walking slowly, pausing to admire the flowerbeds.

What do these women have to do with her? Nothing. They are not even who they seem to be. Mrs. Price has died, so the woman ahead bent over the pansies is surely not Mrs. Price. It is some other woman, who looks like her, who walks like her. And Lulu Mercer, who is she? My mother, my daughter, Gordon's voice says, but Lulu Mercer is neither of these. She is . . . well, what is she? Mrs. Fayer is a practical woman who has no time left for mysteries. Her life is a fact, not a riddle, and it is almost over. It is too late for mysteries; what she cannot understand, she must ignore, she thinks, and get on with the business of living. Mystery means no more to her at this point than—than what?—than that foolish parasol.

The women have cut diagonally through the Garden and are waiting to cross over to Charles Street. The light turns and Mrs. Fayer sees them step out into the street, sees the sun catch the metal tip of the parasol and turn it into a disc of fire before her eyes.

Yes, she will follow them. She leaves the path, hurrying now, and cuts across the grass toward a patch of low shrubs. She is about to go around it and then sees, yes, she will save time by cutting straight through. She pushes the stubby branches aside, one bush, then the others, and then she is almost out. But her purse has caught and she has to tug at the branch to get it free. Finally the tip of the branch breaks and the handle comes loose, but Mrs. Fayer cannot move, because there at her feet, tangled in a coil of green and gold, is a snake. It writhes upon itself and she cannot take her eyes off it. She does not run, she does not cry out. She only stands there, waiting. And then she sees that it is not one snake, but two, and they are not coiled to strike; they are coiled, endlessly it seems, around each other. The thought strikes her like a hammerblow; they are . . . making love. For a second she thinks of crushing them with her foot, of stomping them to bloody pulp.

As Lulu Mercer would, she thinks, and begins to understand.

She must find the women. She has to. Everything depends upon it. She hurries after them.

At the corner of Charles Street, she realizes she has lost them, and the pain is worse beneath her ribs. The light is red and she waits for it to turn.

But she will find them eventually, she is certain of that now.

20

Snow is falling on Marlborough Street. It is dusk and the snowflakes glisten in the pale air. The small front gardens that divide the street from the old stone townhouses are ruined now, and dusted white. It is the first snowfall. The gasflares glow a yellow-green in the old fashioned iron lamps and the snow against the glass goes yellow for an instant before it falls, white, to the ground. Cars move slowly, cautiously, along the broad street. There is no sound.

Mrs. Fayer sits in the bay window of her living room looking out on the street below. This is her favorite hour, the time just before dark when the air is violet and the roofs of the townhouses across the street stand out stark against the sky. And now snow is falling and there are lemon colored pools of light beneath the lampposts.

It is December, 1970, and Mrs. Fayer is beginning her new life. It is not the life she intended when she left Hillside, angry, fed up. It is a different life, one she could not have imagined for herself. It has begun with her heart attack.

Mrs. Fayer looks around her tiny furnished apartment. Nothing in it is hers and yet everything has grown to be hers. Even the plants, which somehow flourish in the hot dry air: African violets, a miniature orange tree, the long fronds of a sword fern. She has never been able to grow anything—the delphinium died long before she was released from the hospital—but now all her plants grow and bloom, even in December.

The apartment itself is modern Gothic, so Gordon says. The carpet is tweed, gold and rust colored, and there is a large formless sofa of rust that goes with it. Chairs stand on either side of the marble fireplace; one a deep chocolate, shapeless also, and the other a high-backed Spanish chair, heavy with carving and upholstered in gold brocade. There are bookcases and end tables and in the bay window a dining table that folds out to seat six. The tiny bedroom is what she has always known: bed, chest, a writing desk. The kitchen and the bathroom are closets that have been converted. None of this furniture, none of these rooms, are hers; she chose them because they happened to be offered to her; and yet she has made them her own.

Mrs. Fayer sits at the table in the bay window, happy, looking down at the soundless street and the people hurrying home, their heads bent against the snow, their shoulders rounded. Each one is going home to a family, a husband, a lover perhaps. And then she sees Gordon.

He is walking slowly, despite the snow, and his head is not bent. He carries his briefcase in his left hand and with his right he cradles a brown shopping bag against his chest. His hair, as she watches from the window, blows back from his forehead in the light wind and he pauses to hoist the bag higher in his arm. She smiles to herself. Gordon is her friend.

Mrs. Fayer and Gordon Sloane have been friends for many months now. He is an eye doctor, a surgeon, and three times a week he performs intricate and dangerous operations that allow people to see again. He is well known throughout the city as the man to handle the almost impossible vision problems: cases are referred to him from Mass. General and from the Lahey Clinic. At fifty, he is tall and trim, a small bulge just beginning to show around his middle. From a distance he looks thirty, a look he cultivates with a light bronzing cream he applies even in December and with his carefully styled hair, which is silver and very thick. He has small perfect features and eyes that are so light a brown they sometimes look yellow. Wrinkles have begun to appear around his eyes and mouth, and the skin at his jaw is slack. But he dresses expensively and in the latest style; his nurses never fail to comment on how well he looks.

Gordon Sloane lives on the floor above Mrs. Fayer; his apartment, unlike her own, runs the full depth of the building. It is sparely decorated in deep blues and browns and white; a very masculine, very elegant apartment full of light and space. They never meet at Gordon's, but always in Mrs. Fayer's modern Gothic living room, and they have been meeting each day now for months.

Their friendship began when Mrs. Fayer returned from the hospital after her heart attack. Almost every day it seemed—either at the mailboxes or in the elevator—she would run into Gordon and the woman she took to be his wife. And always they would greet one another, pleasantly, a little remote. Mrs. Fayer thought them a handsome couple; it made her glad to see them. There was something about Gordon that reminded her of Dr. Turner, a gentleness, a kind of deference that was almost shyness.

Dr. Turner was often in her mind these days. She had failed him and failed herself too. And out of what? Was it fear? Or selfishness? She had kept something back, because . . . why? Was it the risk of failing him, of being found out? No, Eugene was not right. She was not a destroyer. She could have been something for Dr. Turner; she could have made some kind of life with him. "I have failed you," she would say aloud and force herself to think of other things. But seeing Gordon always brought her mind back to Dr. Turner and how different their lives might have been.

And then one day in September, Mrs. Fayer and Gordon met at the front door, she with a shopping bag from Bonwit's, he with his leather briefcase, and he said to her, "Gin and tonic weather." He mopped his forehead with a handkerchief and then fiddled with his mailbox key, trying to get it into the lock. "Yes," she said, and then, "Why don't you stop by and have it with me?" Gordon paused in shuffling through his mail. "And your wife, of course," she added just as he said, "I will. Yes. Thank you." And they took the elevator to Mrs. Fayer's apartment.

And so they are back in that present, in September.

As she slices the lime and measures out the gin, she wonders why he has not gone upstairs to get his wife. "Do you want to call her?" she says finally, "or do you just want to nip upstairs and get her?"

"Her?"

"Your wife."

"Oh, Jeanne," he says, understanding now. "I'm not married. Jeanne is, well, just a friend. She's an old friend."

Now what? Has she done the wrong thing? Has she been too forward?

"Dr. Sloane," she says. "You must excuse me. I didn't know. It's just that I've seen you together and presumed . . . stupid of me."

She hands him the glass; it is too late now to withdraw the invitation.

"No," he says, "I'm not."

They talk about the heat in Boston during September, the terrible cold of winter; they exhaust the weather. Mrs. Fayer seems him now as she has not seen him before; he is not young, after all, he is not . . . what? . . . happy? His eyes are almost yellow in this room; they are wary eyes, they are on guard.

"Tell me what you do," she says. "I always see you with that briefcase, but I know from your letterbox that you're a doctor."

"I'm an eye doctor," he says. "In surgery." And, though he has never done this before, because it surely must be boring, he explains to Mrs. Fayer the intricacy of eye surgery, the kinds of cases which can be salvaged and the kinds which are hopeless. He tells her about experiments being made to give sight to the totally blind. He has forgotten the time and the heat. He is talking about something near and precious to him, something that gives his life the only meaning it has. The eye. Vision. And she listens and nods and asks intelligent questions. But she does more than this. What does she do? What is it she is asking from him and, at the same time, making it easy for him to give?

She has the most extraordinary eyes—green, a pure deep green, with gold flecks at the limbus. They are a child's eyes, wide and defenseless. He could love her. He could trust her. He smiles suddenly, thinking to himself, I must be going mad.

He has finished his drink, but he cannot go yet until he has asked about her. He has talked only about himself.

"May I get you another?" she says.

"If I'm not keeping you," he says.

And so she fixes him another drink.

"I'm embarrassed," he says. "We've talked so much about me—or rather, I have. That's really very rude, isn't it. Tell me about you. You'll *have* to tell me, just to keep me from feeling I've been an awful bore."

They talk about her then, a widow, retired.

Whatever it is he expected, or hoped for, he must hear in the plain story she tells him. He is moved, touched. Yes, he could trust her. Perhaps some day she'll be the one he will tell. But it is late now and he puts down his drink, firmly, and says that he really should go.

"I'm sorry if I've stayed too long."

"No. Oh no," she says. "It's been so long since I've talked."

"Me too," he says. "I've enjoyed it."

But he does not get up to leave. They have had a personal conversation, but no more personal than any two strangers meeting on a train might have. Nothing embarrassing has been said. There has been no baring of the soul. Why, then, does this seem so intimate, so confidential a moment? Perhaps it is his exhaustion. Perhaps it is the summer heat that has worn him down and is about to devastate him.

Whatever the explanation, he does not get up and leave. He does not take that one moment when he might keep his life in his own hands, safe, and walk out the door and be done with her, a woman of seventy, who has known nothing of life and has no right to share his. He does not leave. He sits there on her rust colored couch, his elbows resting on his knees, his chin resting on his folded hands, and the voice he hears speaking is his own.

"I am a homosexual," he says.

And so it is said at last.

Gordon Sloane is fifty years old and he has never said these words to anyone. He is a homosexual: this is his secret, this is his most unspeakable self. And now he has spoken it and waits for Mrs. Fayer's response.

But she makes no response. She only looks at him, frankly, as if she has known this secret for years.

"I've never told anyone that," he says. "You're the first person I've ever told."

"Then thank you," she says, "for trusting me."

"I don't know why. I didn't intend to tell you . . . to tell anyone . . . ever." He draws a deep breath and then exhales slowly. "I'm sorry if . . ."

"It's something I understand," she says, looking at him but seeing Jessie Price instead. "I have a friend, a student. She's a philosopher actually." But she stops because she realizes he is not listening.

"All these years," he says, "fearing it and wanting it, and poor Jeanne not knowing what I was, what I *am;* she never guessed; no one did. A homosexual." He says it bitterly, as if he is punishing himself with the word.

"Does it matter that much? That you are homosexual?" She is looking for other words, for the right ones.

"Can I have another drink?" he says.

"Yes, of course," she says. But before she gets him the drink, she finds the words she has been looking for. "But what difference does it make," she says, "to love women or men? We are who we are, in the end. Don't you agree? So what does it matter?"

"The drink?" he says. And as she fixes it, he tells her how much it has mattered, how much it matters still. He goes on and on, and she is careful to say little, to say nothing eventually, only nodding and agreeing with whatever he says.

Finally his intensity slackens, he is embarrassed, his eyes grow wary again. They talk about the city, about the antique shops. And then at last he goes, and Mrs. Fayer thinks to herself that this is the last she will see of him, that in the morning he will realize what he has said, and will avoid her in the future. But she is only partly right.

In the morning he determines to avoid her at whatever cost; he even considers moving out of his apartment. But by lunch time, the full awareness of what he has done descends upon him, and his reaction is a very mixed one. He has handed over his reputation to a stranger, true, but she might well be a harmless stranger and furthermore there is a certain satisfaction in having finally said it. "I am a homosexual." In a way, he thinks, saying the words has made him free. The afternoon passes quickly with rounds of conferences and paper work and the constant thought, I have told somebody. Someone knows.

Someone knows and has not rejected him. He bounds up the stairs after work, eager to see her again, this Mrs. Fayer, to discover if he has put himself in a trap or, by some ironic twist, set himself free.

"Come in," she says. "What a pleasant surprise!" She busies herself making him a drink while he invents casual topics of conversation: an amusing story from the hospital, the lady who feeds pigeons in the Public Garden, the weather.

But she too has prepared, just in case.

"We were talking about antique shops the other night," she says. "I'm looking for a clock to put on the mantelpiece. I always like a clock on the mantel."

"An antique clock?" he asks.

"I thought perhaps one of those glass-fronted ones, where you can see all the mechanisms turning. I like those. I like to look at them." She smiles suddenly. "When you haven't got much time left, you like to keep an eye on it."

So. She has a sense of humor. A good sign.

"The clock shop on Charles Street would be the place to try," he says. "They've got every kind of clock ever made, I think. Antiques, rare art works, and junk. Take your pick; it's all there."

"The clock shop," she says. "Is that what it's called?"

"Well, no. But it's got this big clock—huge, it is—hanging over the door. You can't miss it."

And so they talk a while longer about clocks and antiques. Mrs. Fayer is polite and chatty and relaxed; she gives no sign that she knows his secret, that she looks at him with a different eye.

Yes, he is safe with her.

"Got to go," he says. "I'm meeting Jeanne for dinner."

He bounces up the stairs to his own apartment, relaxed, but on guard still.

A week goes by and Gordon is having a drink with Mrs. Fayer once again. He has called from work to ask if he might stop by and now, in her living room, he shifts uneasily from foot to foot as they talk about her new clock. It has a transparent case and they stand before the mantel watching the hundreds of tiny wheels turn round and round, interlocking for a second, for a fraction of a second, and then moving on in an eternal circle.

"Fascinating," he says.

"Yes, you can have grim thoughts or pleasant thoughts looking at that. I've had both, already."

They touch glasses.

"To the new clock," he says.

"To pleasant thoughts," she says.

But in less than twenty minutes he says what has been on his mind. "You can't imagine what it was like, knowing what

I was and wanting someone and not being able to . . . It would get so bad sometimes that I'd go down to the river and get picked up."

"Our dark sides," she says.

"It was . . . What do you mean, 'our dark sides'? You're so gnomic. You're like a sybil." He leans toward her and his eyes burn a deep yellow.

"I meant merely that all of us have a side we rarely have to confront, a side we're rarely fortunate enough to confront."

"That's what I thought you meant. But I wondered." He takes a sip of his drink and his mind wanders away once more, back to the river. "It was suicidal, it really was." He gets up and paces the room, stopping in front of the mantel, his back to Mrs. Fayer. "Can I tell you?" he says. "Do you find it shocking?"

"*Humanus sum,*" she says, but he is not listening. "Sorry. No, of course not; it doesn't shock me."

"It would be like this. I'd be very tired from work and on the way home I'd stop at a bar and have a few drinks, just lingering there, you know, looking available. And somebody, some guy, would always start a conversation, and then his voice would drop and the tone would change, and he'd say something like, 'How about it?' or more often, 'How about picking up a couple of broads?' And I'd always plead business or a date or something. Something proper, something unarguable. And then home, here," he points to the ceiling, "where I'd pace up and down the apartment, drinking, just waiting to go unconscious. Oh, I should tell you, always on a night when I wasn't operating the next morning." He laughs, a disdainful laugh, dismissive. "And then, around midnight, something would always happen, as I knew it would, of course, because it had become a pattern. My pulse would accelerate, but there'd be a surface of calm over the hypertension, and I'd go to the closet and get a pair of chinos and a white sweater and I'd put them on. And then I'd go down to Arlington Street and across the overpass, and I'd walk around the amphitheatre and the lagoon and the boat dock. There are always plenty of them there—fags in chinos and sweaters. And finally I'd sit on one of the benches down by the lagoon, you know where the trees hide them almost completely, and I'd light up a cigarette and wait. It was insane, it really was. Anyone could have seen me. I could've been arrested, you know what the cops here are like, and they patrol that place in a cruiser all night long. Even while I was sitting there, waiting, I could see headlines in the newspapers, 'Local doctor charged with soliciting.' Or I could have been mugged or murdered or anything. And eventually somebody would come along, walk past the bench, and then turn around and come back and say, 'Do you mind if I share your bench?' and I'd say, 'Help yourself,' and then he'd say something about the weather, and then your knees would touch, accidentally, only for a second, and you don't pull away, and then his hand slips over onto your thigh. I'll never forget the first time. I kept thinking, this can't be happening, this isn't me. It was as if I was standing outside of myself watching it happen to somebody else. I remember laughing. I laughed right out loud and the guy was offended. It was insane. I came home, I remember, and drank nearly a pint of bourbon until I went unconscious. The next morning I was still shaking from it, and I vowed it would never happen again, never. And the next night I went back for more."

He has been talking wildly, his hands agitated and his eyes darting from Mrs. Fayer to the bay window and back. He pauses now, waiting for some response.

"We don't seem to learn much from experience, do we," she says, and it is enough; he goes on.

"I haven't done that for years now, for two years to be exact. But I've thought about it a lot, about what it means. And you know I've come to the conclusion—I suppose it's obvious really—that I was *trying* to get myself caught. By a cop or by a mugger or a dope addict or something. I think

I wanted to be found out. Maybe to punish myself for being homosexual. Do you think so?"

"I've never been able to figure out why we do the things we do. The destructive things."

They are silent then and he begins to hear the words he has been telling her. He flushes.

"Do I disgust you?" he says. "Do you think I'm . . ."

"I think you're a good person who's been . . . unhappy."

"Unhappy, yes. Good, I'm not so sure."

"All of us, everybody, have things we've done that make us wake up in the night and cover our faces. Don't you think that's so?"

"Do *you?*" he says.

"Yes, I do."

"Like what?"

She thinks for only a second; there can be no refusing him. "I was unfaithful to my husband once. And . . . there are other things."

"You've been married." He says it flatly; it is something he cannot understand, he cannot get over.

"Not very happily, I'm afraid."

"But you've done it, you see. At least you've done it."

"Well, yes."

"I've thought of marrying. Jeanne would like to, you know."

"From what you've said, I think you were wise not to."

"No, that's the problem. I couldn't. I'd be afraid."

"The dark at the top of the stairs."

He is silent then, and after a while they talk about neutral subjects, about the hospital, about her clock again. And then he goes.

He trusts her now. They have settled into a comfortable relationship. They are friends, they are like brother and sister. With her, he forgets he is a homosexual.

And now it is the present, December, and months have passed since they first became friends. Gordon stops in on his way from work and they talk, for a few minutes at least, almost every day. Sometimes he stays for a drink and sometimes he stays for dinner or takes her out to dinner. Sometimes Jeanne joins them and all three go out together, although Gordon has been seeing less of Jeanne these past weeks. Mrs. Fayer watches him turn into the walk and knows he will stop at her door to say it's snowing.

Mrs. Fayer hears the elevator stop and she hears him put down the shopping bag, but he does not knock. She clicks on the overhead light and waits. Still no knock. She opens the door and he is there, head turned away, arm stretched out stiff, holding a small bunch of roses.

"I, gee, I uh, brung you dese flowers, Missus Fayer."

"Kind suh," she says. "Ah am not worthy of your attentions. Ah will, howevah, accept one perfect rose." She takes the flowers quickly, because she knows she is clumsy at this kind of play. "Come in, you big silly, before someone sees you and has you arrested. Look at you, you're all snow."

Gordon stamps his feet on the carpet outside the door and then comes inside and, as he takes off his overcoat, scatters snow everywhere.

"I'm glad to see you," she says, touching his arm. "Never mind the rug."

"Guess what?" He stands, hands on hips, a winner.

"You've been made chief of staff."

He stands there, beaming at her.

"Oh Gordon, really? Have you?"

"No less," he says.

"Oh I'm glad. I'm so glad for you."

"And so, Madame, *est-ce que je peux avoir le plaisir de votre* . . . I forget what company is. *Compagnie?* Let's go to dinner, Jessie. Okay?"

"I'd love it," she says, and adds at once. "But what about Jeanne? Don't you think she'd like to . . . I mean, wouldn't you rather have dinner with her?"

Mrs. Fayer is fixing the roses in a fluted vase when he comes to her and, bending down, kisses her on the forehead.

"Us," he says. "Let's just have it be us, Jessie."

She glances up at him and smiles.

"Us," she says, and turns back to the flowers, bowing her head above them.

Us.

And so she is in love with him.

Gordon Sloane is fifty; he could be her son. Mrs. Fayer tells herself this as she walks beside him down Marlborough Street. He is tall and handsome, courtly to her. How is it that she has been a nun in a convent, a life of prayer and penance stretching ahead of her, and now she is walking down Marlborough Street on the arm of a handsome man? She is going to a French restaurant, the DuBarry, where she will drink wine and make conversation. And she, seventy years old. How can this be?

She has read somewhere that the thing most feared in secret always happens. She did not know what it meant, but it has stayed with her. Is this what she has feared? It makes no sense.

He could be my son, she tells herself, as she walks by his side. I love him like a son.

And as he leans across the table to pour her wine, she studies for the thousandth time the way the black hairs at his wrist curl up from his shirt cuff. She always wants to stroke his wrist, just there, where the hairs stop. She wants to kiss him there.

He could be my son, she tells herself.

"It could have been so different, couldn't it?" he says.

Does he know what she is thinking?

"What could?"

"Us. Our lives." He is leaning toward her now, talking softly, intently. "If we had met . . . oh God . . . before all the things that have happened to us *did* happen to us. Before you went into the convent, and before I . . . well, you know."

"But look what we have," she says, and opens her hands to include the table and the two of them.

"Yes, but it could have been different."

They stop talking while the waiter takes their plates.

"I wouldn't want it different. This is perfect. If I could, I'd make time stop completely and just live forever in the present moment. Do you know what I mean?"

"You mean you're happy."

She laughs, because of course that is exactly what she means. She had thought she was saying something more complicated.

"I remember once when I was a child, about twelve, I suppose, I remember walking with a nun whose name was Sister Veronica and another little girl, Ruth. And we were walking on either side of this nun; we were going up a gravel path, white gravel, to the cemetery which was on a little hill. When we got to the gate we stopped and rested under a huge elm tree. And I remember that. I remember I wanted to make time stop and just live in that moment forever. And I guess I did, in a way."

She is transformed; she grows radiant as she talks.

"I was in love then too," she says.

He is staring at her, this woman old enough to be his mother. Jessica Fayer. Jessica Fayer. He says the name over and over to himself. For a second the panic rises in him: she is a woman, she will want to be loved, she will want to be held. She is an invader, a destroyer. But then their eyes catch and hold. No, she is only Jessica Fayer. She is a friend. He is not afraid of her.

"I'm not afraid of you," he says finally. It has taken him an hour to decide to say it, and now they are seated on the rust colored couch in Mrs. Fayer's apartment on Marlborough Street.

"That's good," she says. "I'm not very frightening anyway."

"I guess it's because you've accepted me."

"Maybe it's because you've accepted yourself."

"No. I'll never accept *that* part of me."

She puts down her brandy glass and touches his wrist just below the shirt cuff.

"What?" he says.

"Nothing. That's sweet, there."

He looks into her eyes, but she is looking at his wrist. He can stop all this now. It is not too late. He can laugh and pull his hand away. He can get up and pour some more brandy. He can break this moment.

"Would you mind?" he says, and he gets up and then stretches out full length on the couch, with his head in her lap. "Jessica Fayer," he says, and he aches in his groin.

She strokes his hair, thick and silver, her long thin fingers running through it, slowly, gently. His head is hot and his neck tense against her thigh.

She does not say, I love you. She will not do that to him. She will not do anything to change this moment, to lose this tremendous intimacy. No one has ever trusted her so much. No one has ever given her so much. She must not say, I love you. And yet, why not? She will give him this, unasked.

"I love you," she says.

"Would you?" he begins, and then stops. And then it is like the time he told her he was a homosexual; he hears the voice and knows that he must have spoken. "Would you lie down with me? Here?"

"Yes," she says, and so they are there, stretched out together on the couch, arms around one another. Her face is crushed against his chest; she can feel his heart pounding.

"I love you," he says.

She feels him grow hard against her. No, she is not imagining it.

"I'm sorry," he says, and leans away from her slightly.

"That's all right," she says. "It's nice."

She moves her hip and her knee so that their two bodies fit together more easily.

"I could do it," he says. "I really could."

"Yes." She holds him tight. She does not want to think. She does not want to lose this moment.

"Can I? I want to."

"We'll lose everything," she says, but already she has surrendered. Already she has taken him into herself.

"I can," he says. "I want to."

They do not speak any more. She is careful to let him lead. No more darkness at the top of the stairs, she thinks, and it is her last thought. She gives herself up to love; to another person. She is loved. She is giving love. Her eyes grow deep green and glassy, as he looks into them, smiling.

"I did it," he says. "Oh my God, I love you, Jessie." He collapses against her, pulling her tight to him. I'm free, he says to himself, I'm free at last.

"Love," she says. "Yes."

She does not know what love is. Has she done this for love? Has she destroyed whatever it was they had together by this one unthinking act? She lies against him, silent, and the only sound in the room is the ticking of the mantel clock as the hundreds of tiny wheels turn and turn. Finally, she must ask him.

"You don't think I'm . . . grotesque?"

"Grotesque! Oh Jessie, Jessie! You've just set me free. God no, not grotesque. Anything but grotesque. I love you."

I love you, Gordon Sloane has said, and he means it.

In the spring he will marry, but he will go on loving Jessica Fayer, in his way. He will marry because he can, and —he thinks—must, but he will not marry Jeanne, who has waited for him for twenty years. He will marry Diane Curtis, who is thirty and divorced, and who is the daughter of a distinguished and wealthy Beacon Hill family. Jessica Fayer will be the godmother of his first child, whom he will name after her: Jessica Curtis Sloane.

And what about Jessica Fayer?

"All human loves do not end," she says, sitting at her bay window or walking through the Public Garden, wondering what kind of love this was, this *is,* that lasted for only a minute or two and yet continues to live. And then she tells herself to be glad she has it, whatever it is. "Sister Veronica was wrong," she says. "There *is* love; love at the end.

The thing most feared in secret has happened at last.

21

Mrs. Fayer is nearly out of time. She sits on a bench in Louisburg Square, gathering her strength to pursue Mrs. Price and Lulu Mercer. Her pocketbook with the torn photographs and holy cards lies on the bench beside her. Her hands are folded in her lap.

The sun has fallen below the line of buildings and a small breeze has come up, refreshing her. She can continue now to the end.

As she rises from the bench she hears the squeal of tires and the roar of a powerful motor. It is them, she knows. And yes, in a minute the huge green Mercedes rockets up the hill, Adam at the wheel and Martha next to him. When it is dark, they will pick up some boys. Mrs. Fayer shakes her head. No. She sits down on the bench once more, just for a moment, just until she feels more like herself.

How many hours pass? Does she nod off? Perhaps she returns to that present where she walks with Sister Veronica and listens to her rich hypnotic voice. "All human loves end. His love is fire." Or to that present where, forever, Virgil Clark carries her down the stairs, naked, their black and white limbs twining. Or to the hospital and Eugene, smiling at her, saying, "I need you." There is no way of knowing. But when she finally rises from the bench, night has fallen and there is only a pale wedge of moon to see by.

Mrs. Fayer stands and looks around her for a moment. She must decide which way to go. She leaves her pocketbook lying on the bench; she will have no more need of that. She must be free, unencumbered by anything. She decides to go further up the hill.

But this is foolish, looking for these two women. Jessie Price is dead; she has been gone for two years now. And Lulu Mercer? Mrs. Fayer wonders for a moment if Lulu Mercer really exists. I'm old and dotty, she thinks, but not that dotty. She has seen them at the Top Of The Hub. And she has seen them again this afternoon; Mrs. Price had held a white parasol; yes, she has seen them. She will find them. But why?

There are bells suddenly. Mrs. Fayer counts them. Ten. It is ten o'clock and she is wandering alone on Beacon Hill.

It is ten o'clock and Adam Brockway has pulled his car up to the curb where the two young men stand waiting. They have been taken once again. They have spent Mrs. Fayer's money on grass and discovered too late that what they bought was indeed grass. So now they are out of money and have to start over. But they are young and confident; they've got all the time in the world. Something will turn up.

Adam pulls his car up to the curb.

"Hi, y'all," Martha calls to them.

The two young men know about Martha and Adam; they have gone for drives with them twice before. Martha is the hophead Adam uses to get his boys. Adam is on speed all the time. The only way he can get off is to have some kid blow him while he's tearing along the highway. It's okay. It's kind of wild. The two young men approach the car.

"How 'bout a fast ride in a nice car," Martha says, her eyes out of focus, glassy with the drug.

"How much?"

"Twenty," she says.

"Fuck it."

"Fifty," Adam says. He has millions now. What is the difference between twenty and fifty? He's almost ready. He can feel the highway rushing beneath his car, his head is back, he is floating. He's going to find it. He's going to find it in the next minute. It's right around the next corner. He wants to come. "Fifty," he says again, "each."

They start to get into the back seat, but Adam says no, and then Martha gets in back with one of the boys and the other one gets in beside Adam.

The heavy car pulls away from the curb and on to Charles Street and then on to Storrow Drive. They will circle on to Memorial Drive and end up again on Beacon Hill. As they pick up speed, Adam tugs at his zipper and says, "Come on. And make sure it's the ride of my life."

It is the last ride of his life. He will be found dead in less than an hour, the transmission of the Mercedes driven up through the front seat, crushing to death the two young men, the beautiful black girl, and the driver. Their limbs are all tangled together and it is some time before the bodies can be identified. This is not true, however, of the old woman who lies dead near the wreckage, a parasol by her side. She is composed, there is no spot of blood on her, only the faint trace of a smile upon her lips. But that is not now, that is not the present. In the present Adam is going faster and faster along Storrow Drive and Mrs. Fayer, exhausted and almost done, turns up streets and down streets, without direction, without sense, determined to find what she is looking for in the maze of Beacon Hill.

She has just begun to despair of ever finding them, when she turns into a little alley marked "dead end" and sees the two women standing beneath a doorlamp. Yes, she is sure it is they.

And they cannot escape her this time, because there is no way out. The brick walls of back gardens rise on either side, and at the head of the alley there is the rear wall of St. Stephen's Church, sheer stone five stories high.

The two women stand under a little lamp by a door. They are quarreling. One of them, Lulu Mercer, snatches the parasol from Mrs. Price, who tries to wrench it back. Lulu Mercer is shouting at her, angry words tumbling from her mouth, but none of them are intelligible. And then she begins to beat Mrs. Price with the parasol, bringing it hard down upon her shoulders and breasts. Neither woman is saying anything now, the only sound is the slashing of the parasol against bone and flesh.

"Stop. Stop that." Mrs. Fayer lunges at the parasol, but Lulu Mercer pulls it free and hides it behind her.

This is madness. This cannot be happening. And yet she sees those tiny eyes and the insane curls bobbing along the forehead. So it *is* happening after all. It is the only present left.

"Why? Why?" Mrs. Fayer is near tears.

"She took my umbrella," Lulu Mercer says. "She's a thief. She's a no-good. Her tongue should be torn out."

There must be some other present. Gordon? Eugene? No.

"Whose umbrella is it?"

Lulu Mercer and Mrs. Price glance at one another and say nothing. After a moment Lulu Mercer puts up her hand and they whisper behind it.

"It's our umbrella," Lulu Mercer says.

"It's our umbrella," Mrs. Price says.

"Won't you accept it?" they say together.

Ridiculous. Absurd.

And yet without a word she takes the parasol, which is white with a ruffle all around the edge, and she pushes it open, and places it above her head.

"Judith."

"Mrs. Fayer."

"Jessica," she says. "I'm Jessica Fayer."

Jessica Fayer is in the present, an old woman with a parasol above her head, as she turns away from Lulu Mercer and Mrs. Price, who are already fading into the insubstantial dark. It is done now. She has accomplished whatever it was she had to do. There is a smile of deep peace on her face.

Jessica Fayer is turned toward the light, the headlights of

the heavy car that crests the hill now, as it must, and turns into the alley, accelerating all the while. But it is not the car lights that she sees; it is a smaller light, and distant. And she will get to it. She will get to it in the minute beyond this one.

But this is the minute she is in.

Jessica Fayer, her head high, her ruffled parasol tilted on her shoulder, walks in the present and forever toward that tiny distant light, full of the joy of this moment.

FOR THE BEST IN PAPERBACKS, LOOK FOR THE 

In every corner of the world, on every subject under the sun, Penguin represents quality and variety—the very best in publishing today.

For complete information about books available from Penguin—including Pelicans, Puffins, Peregrines, and Penguin Classics—and how to order them, write to us at the appropriate address below. Please note that for copyright reasons the selection of books varies from country to country.

In the United Kingdom: For a complete list of books available from Penguin in the U.K., please write to *Dept E.P., Penguin Books Ltd, Harmondsworth, Middlesex, UB7 0DA*.

In the United States: For a complete list of books available from Penguin in the U.S., please write to *Dept BA, Penguin*, Box 120, Bergenfield, New Jersey 07621-0120.

In Canada: For a complete list of books available from Penguin in Canada, please write to *Penguin Books Canada Ltd, 10 Alcorn Avenue, Suite 300, Toronto, Ontario, Canada M4V 3B2*.

In Australia: For a complete list of books available from Penguin in Australia, please write to the *Marketing Department, Penguin Books Ltd, P.O. Box 257, Ringwood, Victoria 3134*.

In New Zealand: For a complete list of books available from Penguin in New Zealand, please write to the *Marketing Department, Penguin Books (NZ) Ltd, Private Bag, Takapuna, Auckland 9*.

In India: For a complete list of books available from Penguin, please write to *Penguin Overseas Ltd, 706 Eros Apartments, 56 Nehru Place, New Delhi, 110019*.

In Holland: For a complete list of books available from Penguin in Holland, please write to *Penguin Books Nederland B.V., Postbus 195, NL-1380AD Weesp, Netherlands*.

In Germany: For a complete list of books available from Penguin, please write to *Penguin Books Ltd, Friedrichstrasse 10-12, D-6000 Frankfurt Main I, Federal Republic of Germany*.

In Spain: For a complete list of books available from Penguin in Spain, please write to *Longman, Penguin España, Calle San Nicolas 15, E-28013 Madrid, Spain*.

In Japan: For a complete list of books available from Penguin in Japan, please write to *Longman Penguin Japan Co Ltd, Yamaguchi Building, 2-12-9 Kanda Jimbocho, Chiyoda-Ku, Tokyo 101, Japan*.